THE WHEELHOUSE CAFÉ

—a love story in the key of sea

Dear Pramila
May you always stay anchored to what's true...

iBooks
Habent Sua Fata Libelli

iBooks

Manhanset House
Dering Harbor, New York 11965
Tel: 212-427-7139
bricktower@aol.com • www.ibooksinc.com

Library of Congress Cataloging-in-Publication Data
The Wheelhouse Café, a love story in the key of sea
Lieblien, Yvonne. p. cm.

1. Fiction—General 2. Fiction—Adventure 3. Fiction—Sea Stories
Fiction, I. Title.

978-1-59687-439-8, Hardcover
978-1-59687-440-4, Trade Paper

First Edition
First Printing

THE WHEELHOUSE CAFÉ

—a love story in the key of sea

Yvonne Lieblein

Dedication

Immense gratitude & much love to my stalwart crew
—Josh, Schuyler, Justus, Melania, & Lynette

"I'm just a sailor, dear,
and I'm torn between the tides.
There's a raging sea
that's got a hold of me,
and the woman on my mind."

—Captain John Raymond

The Wheelhouse Café is anchored by a songscape.
Visit *thewheelhousecafe.com* to amplify your
experience before, after, or while you read.

Prologue: Captain John Raymond

Tuesday, May 10, 1994

Sometimes there's no difference between sea and sky. Gray meets gray at the horizon, a bland backdrop to mirror a monotonous tow. Today, I'm grateful a colorless seascape envelops the *Alanna Rose* as we steam westbound toward the city. I sure as hell don't need the sky to give Long Island Sound any reason to sparkle.

I heard about Billy the same disconnected way I find out about everything on the tug, from a voice coming through the VHF radio. Usually, I imagine each sentence floating into the wheelhouse, suspended in midair, but when I heard *Billy Mickelson*, each word seemed to drop and splatter onto the gray metal deck.

I forget Little Hal is standing nearby until he puts his hands on the wheel, nudging me aside. "That your friend Billy he's talking about? He's on the *Dace?*" Without shifting his eyes, Little Hal picks up his plastic New York Mets cup for a gulp of what I suspect is Fanta Orange, his latest obsession.

"Yeah, it's him." I clench and unclench my fists to loosen up my cramped hands. How long have I been clutching the wheel?

Little Hal is anything but little. He has a tall, wide, don't-fuck-with-me build and is a pro at bobbing and weaving to navigate around the *Alanna Rose* without smacking his head. Salt and pepper curls spring out from the tattered Mets cap that never leaves his head, and he's wearing his usual uniform of putty-colored Carhartts with a faded, red and black buffalo check flannel shirt.

In spite of his massive presence, Little Hal somehow manages to give me space in the wheelhouse. Most of the time I'm here alone, but once in a while someone comes up and annoys the living shit out of me. Little Hal, he doesn't rush to fill the silence, and my appreciation for anyone who knows when to be quiet has crescendoed over the last two decades.

I pick up the VHF mic to hail the *Dace Reinauer*, hoping to find out what the hell happened. I know the Coast Guard has only been searching for a few hours, but I have a prickly feeling Billy's man-overboard story isn't going to have a happy ending.

The *Dace*'s first mate sounds shaken and solemn as he tells me how the night had been a real bruiser, blowing 30 knots out of the east, with 8- to 10-foot seas knocking them around. No one saw Billy go over, but they're guessing that's what happened around 3 or 4 a.m. I cringe as this stranger speaks aloud the thought I've been trying to extinguish since I heard Billy had been swallowed by the sea: "I mean, it's not like he had any reason to jump."

Four in the morning is without a doubt the loneliest time on a tug—a couple of guys on and everyone else already rocked to sleep or trying to get there. Billy and I had talked about those dark hours before dawn and being taunted by what could have been, might have been, and would never be. It felt good to describe the loneliness of waking up scratched and bruised from an onslaught of abrasive thoughts, especially the really cruel fuckers that gave us glimpses of disappointments that were too painful to think about in broad daylight.

I know that if Billy had been really jammed up about something last night, even shitty weather wouldn't have been enough to keep him off the deck. We'd talked too often about that abyss, and how the only remedy was to get out of our racks and out of our heads. Surrounded by cocoons of dark, uncomplicated silence, we'd find small doses of relief in the early morning air.

I stretch out my arms and place each hand on one of the giant panes that make the wheelhouse feel like an oversized fishbowl. Then I lean forward to stare out at the sameness. I close my eyes for a few seconds before reopening them slowly, wishing I'd see Billy off the starboard side, one of his arms wrapped around a bright, orange life ring and the other waving wildly overhead.

I remembered the night last month when we were both in Greenport. Billy had been torn up when we met for a few beers at Whiskey Wind. "This is the one that mattered," he'd said, twirling a cardboard coaster on the bar. "I always thought we'd end up together eventually, like it was inevitable. But let's face it; I spend too much time at sea inside my own fucking head. She's not interested, and she never was Game over."

I hadn't known what to say, so I let shots of mescal do the talking. We'd pretended to watch the Knicks-Nets playoff game, and then I gave him a ride home. No doubt Billy had been feeling battered, but was he banged up enough to jump?

Little Hal taps me on the shoulder. "Hey, Cap, I've got this if you want to split."

I know he doesn't expect me to answer, and I also know he understands that the wheelhouse is the only place I want to be right now. Over the last twenty years, it's become the one place that feels like home.

I grab my almost-empty mug for a swig of coffee. Somehow this shit manages to taste better the longer it sits around. It has real texture now—layers thick enough to yield to my spoon and then cleave to each other again when I stir them up. There's a gritty ring inside, evidence that the tide of coffee has ebbed since I poured it from the shaking silver pot at the beginning of my watch.

I lean over to take my guitar out of its case, lyrics already running through my head. Before I sit, I clutch the VHF mic to make a Wheelhouse Café announcement on Channel 13, the same way I'd broadcast entering a harbor with a deep-loaded oil barge. "Security call. Security call. This is Wheelhouse Café. Wheelhouse Café will be open on Channel 6-8 in five minutes. All interested, switch and listen to Channel 6-8. Wheelhouse Café out."

I clear my throat as I turn our radio to that channel. Little Hal hands me a rubber band so I can key the mic before hanging it from the spotlight handle. "Today's Wheelhouse Café goes out to Billy Mickelson," I say and start to sing "Big Swell,"

"Big swell rolling through the sea,
tumbling on the beach.
Big swell when you're rolling through the ocean,
big swell have mercy on me . . ."

Is anybody listening? Don't know. Never do. There's only one thing I can be sure of as the *Alanna Rose* heads toward New York Harbor—anyone tuning in will know Billy is one of us, and at times like this, we're all just sailors lost at sea.

Chapter One: Arden McHale

Sunday, May 15, 1994

Mother Nature is one heartless bitch.

She could have made the sky a gaping charcoal mouth spewing shards of rain. Instead, she has me wake beneath explosive blue, the blue of my childhood before blue had a name. Then, she punctuates the vivid expanse of color with comma clouds, mocking reminders that the last few days have been a run-on sentence from hell. I don't expect a definitive period or exclamation mark to swoop in and put an end to my confusion. The only punctuation in my future is a nagging question mark.

I don't bother to scan the sky in search of a morning star. I'm no longer a girl who believes in wishes, and even if I did, no wish is going to bring Billy back. He was dead on Tuesday when my mother showed up at my office with a box of tissues and then let me lay across her lap on the Sunrise Bus as I wept all the way from 44th and Third to Greenport. He was dead when I passed out on *Andromeda's* bow late last night with thick sob snot smeared across my face. And he was still dead in those first blurry seconds after the sun pried my eyes open this morning, when my brain was still scrambled enough to wonder if my splitting headache was caused by an ax lodged in my forehead or the drained fifth of vodka in my hand.

Now at least I'm certain it was the vodka, but that's the only thing I'm sure of. I can hear Mom calling my name from the path between our house and the dock. I don't need to wonder how she'll react to finding me sprawled out on the bow of my 21-foot Herreshoff, the fingers of my right hand wrapped around an empty liquor bottle. Mom has spent a lifetime overlooking the obvious to preserve her Pollyanna view of reality. Today won't be any different.

"Arden, honey, I've been looking for you," she half shouts, trying to corral her wayward wisps of ash blonde hair with a flat palm. "Didn't expect you to be up and at 'em so early."

I'm the polar opposite of up and at 'em and completely unable to formulate a cohesive sentence, let alone drum up the energy   to speak. My eyes are still shut, but I know she's looking everywhere but down at me.

"You always seem to lose track of time when you're sailing," she continues, sidestepping my silence with finesse. "It's almost noon already." Another pause. I peek through almost-closed eyelids to see what seems to be a mirage of my mother—transparent, vibrating oil-on-water colors hovering above the dock. Her eyes dart from me, up to the house, down to her watch, and then back to me as she asks, "Do you want to ride with us or do you have other plans?"

"What time . . ." I start, thinking she can't actually believe I've just been leisurely soaking up some May sunshine after a brisk morning sail.

"Two. It's two to four," she interrupts, her words spilling out in the quiet, nervous way they do when she is clutching onto fine with all her might. I tilt my head down to breathe in my makeshift blanket, the faded, navy blue coat Dad left on board after our last sail. Had it really been cold enough to wear a coat the last time I came home for a visit?

"God, I know this is unbearably painful for you," she says, grabbing a starboard cleat for balance as she squats down next to *Andromeda*. "Your eyes are swollen shut, and your face is a crusty mess. Come on in, honey. Take a hot shower. Better yet, a long soak in the tub. You can use the lavender beads you gave me for Mother's Day and . . ."

"Mom, Mom . . . stop. Please." I can't listen any longer. The volume is turned all the way up—colors, sounds, *Andromeda*'s no-longer subtle bob. "I'll be up soon. And remember what I always say: Your daughter will never be a soap opera actress. She only cries one way, and it ain't pretty."

I summon up that shred of humor to give Mom something to hold onto, something to help her believe I'm steady enough for her to turn away from me and follow the path back to our house. She stands up slowly, still hesitant. "Your dad and I plan to get there at two. I imagine there'll be a crowd."

She's right, there will be. I'm not the only one mourning Billy, but I *am* the only one he'd introduced to the half-abandoned, more than a little dangerous shipyard that ignited our childhood imaginations. I'm the only one who understood the *"must-get-out-on-the-water-now"* mantra that propelled him out of bed each morning. I'm also the only one he hadn't spoken to the six weeks before he disappeared, since the night he gave me a pearl bracelet for my birthday and confessed to being in love with me for twenty-six of my thirty years.

And, I'm the only one swept up in a choppy current of guilt, needing to know what might never be known—*why* Billy was lost at sea. Not whether he tripped, slipped, or got swept off the tugboat deck by a rogue wave, but if he chose to jump into the ocean's dark promise of nothingness . . . because of me.

Chapter Two: John

Sunday, May 15, 1994

What's it like to be a tugboat captain? Yeah, you could say I get that a lot. The easy answer goes something like this: My life is days and days of nothing much broken up by moments of sheer adrenalin.

I believe a captain can learn the nuances of every harbor and even figure out how to get from one port to another without losing his barge or his mind, but the ability to shift from monotonous towing to averting disaster? *That's* an innate gift, a skill that can't be taught.

I'll never forget the person who saw that gift in me—Captain Lester Richards. He knew I had it, so he took the time to teach me the ultimate secret to driving massive tons of steel—focus. Lesson number one? The biggest enemy of focus is fear. Lester used to slap my sweat-soaked palms and scream in my ear as he showed me how to look fear in the face and not just face it, but let it combust inside me so it fueled me. Captain Les showed me how to harness fear by breathing through it. *In through the nose. Out through the mouth. Repeat.*

Learning how to respond instead of react took practice, and when I heard the Coast Guard had called off the search and Billy's funeral plans were underway, I was grateful for being able to shut off my emotions and focus. Instead of heading up to Boston with a deep-loaded oil barge, I needed to navigate getting out to Greenport—radio the office for a replacement captain, deliver the barge, and then land the tug at Richmond Terminal Yard on Staten Island. By early Saturday afternoon, I was digging through the barely worn "off-boat" clothes in my closet, trying to locate my lone suit.

It wasn't until early this morning that the molten sadness began to ooze back in. The Midtown Tunnel spit my pickup out onto the Long Island Expressway, a swift reminder that I could always count on the LIE to deliver miles of brutal traffic when I least wanted to be alone.

I roll up in front of Aunt Suebee's cottage nearly three hours later, just in time to watch her pull away from the curb in a powder blue convertible LeBaron, taking my daydreams of a home-cooked dinner with her. That's why I'm eating frozen pizza on her front porch, chuckling at the irony of an almost-eighty-year-old woman hightailing it toward a night on the town while I spend more time alone inside my own fucked-up head.

I'm resigned to hitting the rack early and wouldn't even know who to call if I felt up to a few beers. Except for Aunt Suebee, my entire family has been flying south in small, winter-hating flocks. Any childhood friends who stayed in town are married and caught up in the late-day nets of dinner, baths, and bedtime.

I am the last single man standing. My friends joke about being envious of my perpetual bachelorhood, like it's a never-ending happy hour where cocktails flow and topless women frolic, but I know they're starting to wonder.

Carson routinely encourages me to bust out of the closet. And dozens of failed matchmaking attempts have failed to extinguish Johnny T.'s enthusiasm. He still tries to set me up with his "super hot, *completely* reformed" kleptomaniac cousin from Virginia or the "trust me, she doesn't look old enough to be a grandmother" who helped him restack the pyramid of lentil soup he barreled into at the IGA.

Billy had been different. Not only was he single too—Billy was also the only other Greenporter who made a living as a tugboat captain. The landscape of our lives was almost identical, and he also preferred silence to small talk. Our friendship was forged over sparse conversation and abundant shots of tequila.

I remember being in Greenport one frosty January weekend to make good on my Christmas gift to Aunt Suebee. Billy showed up wanting to know how to get a job on the boats. I took a break from laying tile to walk over to Widow's Hole with him, and he told me he needed to breathe some fresh air before the pasty, oatmeal-colored community college walls suffocated him. I remember saying that if he wanted to be a seaman on a day when the temperature flirted with freezing and a nasty winter wind smacked our faces, then he was crazy enough to work on a tug. Billy had given me a serious nod, and we watched the Shelter Island ferries crisscross the bay a while longer, skipping stones and doing piss-poor imitations of our favorite scenes from Eddie Murphy's *Delirious*.

Billy's family had been less than thrilled with his decision, especially his sister, Clairebeth. She was probably eight or nine when Billy made the switch from commuting to Suffolk for a handful of classes to a schedule that made her an only child for two or three weeks at a time. I remember Billy telling me how his parents' decade-long rumblings escalated into a full-on thunderstorm right before he went to sea, and Clairebeth had accused him of abandoning her.

When I see Billy's parents at the wake, it's clear they've unraveled. When I approach each of them, I know my outstretched hand will be pushed aside for hugs, and we'll nod in sorrowful agreement that there's nothing and everything to say.

Billy's dad is in the back of the room next to a poster-size photo of Billy raising a glistening striped bass overhead. He's huddled in conversation with a woman who's so well put together it looks like she just might fall apart. Billy's mom and her new husband are holding each other up at the front of the room as people lean in, whisper, and shuffle on.

Taking in the family dynamic distracts me from thinking about why I'm in this stale, crowded room until I lock eyes with Billy. It's a photo of him on the Dace, and this Billy is different than the one in the triumphant bass photo, or the Billy in the montage of family snap shots and bad-hair-day school portraits displayed in the hallway. It stings to see him standing on the deck of the *Dace,* the very last place he was alive and well. I keep reminding myself that at least Billy died at home, because I knew he felt the same way about *Dace* as I did about the *Alanna Rose,* but I can't find even a small shred of comfort in that.

Billy and I had talked over the radio more than we actually saw each other in person, and staring at him on the *Dace* reminds me that he used to listen to the Wheelhouse Café whenever our boats were in the same harbor. He especially loved "Coolest Boy," my song about the adventures of a small-town kid whose vulnerability shines through even as he brags his way to being king of all he surveys. More than once, Billy had used a lyric from that song—"Brother, it ain't easy being cool"—at the Whiskey Wind pool table when one of our liquored-up opponents waxed poetic or got belligerent.

Little Hal and Billy are the only people who know I'm the one locking up a VHF channel to perform the Wheelhouse Café, and while Little Hal's stoic expressions make him a kickass poker player, they don't reveal much about his taste in music. Billy, on the other hand, made it no secret that he was a fan.

"John," he'd say, "no *doubt* Wheelhouse Café is genius, all covert and shit. But what the hell do you get out of singing your ass off for nobody?" Pause. "Tell you what, why don't you take that guitar of yours and those fan-fucking-tastic songs of yours and *do something,* man? You could really *be* somebody. It's a damn shame. Would you listen to me? Fuck, now I'm depressing *myself.*" He'd stretched out over the bar to flag down a drink. "Time for another beer."

Billy had been equally subtle about Meredith. He met my ex early on, when she and I were just getting caught up in each other, and then a few times later when someone needed to stick a fork in us because we were done. Once he'd leaned over to whisper, "I don't have any proof, just a feeling right here where it counts." He'd pounded his fist into my gut. "Meredith's got that 'while the cat's away, the mouse will play' vibe, and she's also got you completely fooled. Am I right?"

He was more right than I was ready for. Meredith spent a lot of time and effort trying to hide her true colors. I did an even better job being the dumb ass that chose not to see then, and even though I'd trust Billy's gut with my life, I just didn't want to believe Meredith would cheat on me. When we were together, her need for me seemed almost primal, like she was living a shadow life until I returned to make her whole.

I'm thankful to have Father Henry's entrance and the ensuing find-a-seat shuffle interrupt my stroll down Meredith Lane.   I decide to stay standing in the quick-getaway zone and almost get knocked over by Clairebeth making a beeline to beat Father Henry to the podium. She gives the crowd an extended glimpse of her bright turquoise bra as she leans forward to adjust the microphone and then lets an "Oh, fuck" when it lets out a high-pitched squeak. Cleavage and a well-placed obscenity—she officially has the crowd's undivided attention.

"I think most of you probably know me. I'm Clairebeth, Billy's sister." The room makes a final *swish*. "There's not much you can say when your brother is lost at sea." She pauses, focusing on the crowd and making eye contact with several people. "I bet Billy thinks *we're* the ones lost at sea right now. I mean, he's in a safe harbor. I'm sure of that. We're the ones who have no fucking idea why we're here, what we're supposed to be doing, or where we're headed. When I was a just a little girl, Billy and I ran out into the backyard and there was Dad, squirming around on top of our neighbor, Mrs. Carmichael, on a lawn chair."

I can't see her father's face to gauge his reaction, and thankfully Mrs. Carmichael moved out to Colorado years ago. "They didn't hear us, so they didn't stop. I was terrified," she continues. "What was he *doing* to her? Where was Mom? Billy took my hand and pulled me into the garage. 'Clairebeth,' he said. 'Forget what we just saw. It has nothing to do with us. Let's go inside and have some Italian ice.' Genius. First and foremost, Billy distracted me with my distraction du jour—Italian ice. He also made me feel like everything was going to be OK even though I knew something was very, very wrong. He had the ability to make me feel safe—when we lived together growing up, and then later, when he was fumbling around trying to make his way in the world. I'm not sure what I'm going to do without him. I know it's a nauseating nautical pun, but he was my anchor. Everyone else could be insane or heading that way, but he'd be right there reminding me not to take everything so seriously, that nothing was as bad as it seemed." She exhales, looks toward the EXIT sign, and then heads in that direction with her dad scrambling out behind her.

The room remains motionless until the door clicks shut, and then Billy's mom walks briskly toward the front of the room, talking before she reaches the podium. "Losing Billy has us all churned up, and there's nothing logical or linear about how we grieve or struggle to make sense of something we don't want to accept as real." She appears to be more nervous than flustered as her hands keep touching the twist of blonde hair on the back of her head. "I've got so much to say about Billy, it's hard to know where to begin. As his mother, I witnessed firsthand how he was always giving, giving, giving . . ."

Her voice fades as I sidestep toward the door to escape into the silence of the adjacent room. It appears to be empty, and then I spot a woman with wavy, dark hair perched on the edge of the corner sofa. She's cradling her face in her hands, and as I walk closer, I recognize her. "Arden? Is that you?"

She turns to me, her red-rimmed eyes barely widening with recognition. "John, right?" As she stands up, her lips curve in what is clearly a reflexive attempt to smile politely. I'm surprised at how compact she feels. I lean in to give her a hug and am surprised by how strong she feels, like every part of her is on purpose.

"How come you're in here?" I ask as we sit down.

"I was late and didn't want to interrupt Clairebeth. I was surprised to see her at the podium. How'd she seem to you?"

"She's broken up. That's the only way to describe her. She's never known a world without Billy."

Arden doesn't lift her eyes from the peacock blue swirls on the carpet. "I can barely remember a world without Billy," she says, smoothing the fabric of her black skirt with both hands. "When we were in nursery school, he was riding the teeter-totter like a madman and smacked into me. I don't think he realized I was hurt until he saw me on the ground, convulsing with sobs, and then he jumped right off and held my hand, singing 'Frère Jacques' until our teacher bounded over."

"I'll bet his voice even sucked back then, didn't it?"

"Yeah, even back then," she answers with raised eyebrows and the trace of a smile. "So that's how our friendship started, and it only got weird twenty-five years later."

"Weird?"

"He never mentioned anything to you?" Her smoothing hands are now motionless.

"I haven't talked to him in a while." Ah, *Arden*. The game-over girl.

Billy had talked about Arden a lot, but I hadn't seen her since she was a kid. I remember her from my dad's hardware store, mostly because she used to come in with her mom. I'd thought it was cool that Mrs. McHale was the one buying nails and paint and duct tape. My dad would chat with her about whatever project she had going on, and he always gave Arden a treat—a miniature level or a tiny flashlight key chain.

"So," Arden says, "Billy got me a pearl bracelet for my birthday. And he wrote me a poem. It was all out of the blue and just too much for me." She stops, rubbing her open palms together with her eyes closed. "Anyway, I definitely didn't react the way he wanted me to."

"You mean, you weren't into him?"

"Billy's one of my oldest friends, something I consider to be a hell of a lot more meaningful than being 'into him.' But we're friends, that's all." She winces as though the verb tense slapped her. "I mean, that *was* all."

"He did tell me he had a broken heart. I just didn't . . ."

"Now you know. We weren't even speaking to each other when he went back to the boat this last time. Me and Billy, not talking? Crazy." As she sits up tall and rolls her shoulders back slowly, I notice how her head often tilts a bit to the left, like she's asking a question.

"Listen. You're smart. Billy admitted to me that you're a better sailor than he is. And you're a fox. How could he not fall in love with you, Arden?"

"A fox?"

"A fox. Yes. Foxy," I exhale a sputtering chuckle. "OK, ignore my bad, outdated adjective choice." Tears shine in Arden's grayish blue eyes, but she doesn't cry.

"I *thought* I was like a sister to him. He held my hair back while I puked mint juleps into my neighbor's hedge after our Derby Day party. He even asked my advice on how to break through the Great-Wall-of-Dupris and get Patsy Dupris into bed . . ."

As if summoned by the word "sister" being spoken aloud, Clairebeth slips inside the front door. She closes it quickly, an unsuccessful attempt to leave wisps of pot smoke outside.

"Did you just light up on the front steps?" I ask before I realize my presence isn't even registering in Clairebeth's universe. She is clearly fixated on Arden, and it's evident the weed hadn't been kind enough to tone down the current of raw emotion coursing through her. I can see that Clairebeth's hostility isn't going to be conveyed by her gaze alone.

"So." Clairebeth's voice sounds hollow as she steps away from the door. Her eyes stay locked on Arden, who, I observe with more than just a little concern, appears to have absolutely no "this is a potentially bad, bad situation" radar. I have to resist the urge to fling myself on top of the clueless wonder and roll her toward a foxhole, but I know there's no cover to be found. I have no idea why Clairebeth is all fired up, but she's poised to do some major damage.

"Clairebeth," Arden says, not just standing to meet the red-eyed woman with a zombie-like gait halfway, but also opening her arms as if she's plans to embrace her. "I'm so sorry . . ."

"Don't say it!" Clairebeth bats down Arden's right arm to intercept the incoming hug and then folds her own arms across her chest. "You have no right to be here, Arden McHale. I want you to get the fuck out. *Now.*"

"Clairebeth," I say, stepping between them. "Calm down. Whatever this is, let's stop it now. Everyone's upset." Arden has gone from clueless to confused mess. She isn't crying, but her whole body is trembling, and her bottom lip keeps quivering even after she presses her top teeth into it.

"*Everyone's upset?*" Claire mimics me. "You've got it all wrong, John. *Billy* was upset. Billy was fucking *devastated*. And you know why he's not here, don't you, Arden? I don't mean not here at his fucking *wake*, but not here on this *planet*. Do you need me to say it out loud?"

That does it. Arden darts toward the door, leaving her sweater and handbag behind. I scoop them up from the sofa, relieved Clairebeth doesn't try to tackle Arden or stick a foot out to sabotage her escape attempt.

When Arden's hand lands on the doorknob, she speaks without turning around. "Your brother was my best friend. There's nothing any of us can say or do to bring him back, but we should at least be kind to each other. He would have wanted that."

Open the door. Get out. These commands ricochet through my mind, but they must not make the leap from thought to speech, because Arden remains motionless at the door. Is she still naive enough to think Clairebeth can downshift her anger?

Clairebeth spins around, seemingly unaffected by the fact that Arden isn't looking at her. "There may be nothing any of us can say or do to bring my brother back, my *only* brother back," she says, still keeping her arms crossed. "But, there sure as hell was something *you* could have done when he poured his fucking heart out to you. He told you he loved you. You *ignored* him. But you had a lot of practice ignoring him, didn't you?"

I can see Arden's back rising and falling with her quick breaths. She stays frozen, facing the door as Clairebeth continues, "Admit it. You ignored his feelings for *years* and just when he found the courage to say the words he'd been holding inside since you were kids, what do you do? What any bitchy little I'm-too-good-for-Greenport, I've-got-a-big-job-in-the-city *best friend* who couldn't have a lowly tugboat captain for a boyfriend would do. You made my brother feel lonelier than he thought possible. He told me this, Arden. He. Told. Me. This."

"And you, John" Clairebeth inhales a sob as she turns toward me, "you'd better your distance or you could end up being her next . . ." She stops short and looks beyond me like she's searching for something on the wall behind me. "Do you have any idea how many nights I crouched inside our front window so I could listen to you and Billy talking and laughing on the porch? Sometimes you had your guitar, and when you sang I'd mouth the lyrics along with you. God, I loved "Get in Line." I was just a kid, but I knew it was raunchy long before I looked up *whore* in the dictionary. And "See Your Face?" Liked it so much that I taught myself the chords. First song I ever learned."

I summon a smile and wonder if we're in the eye of Hurricane Clairebeth or the storm has passed? Clairebeth shivers and glares at Arden for a stretched out second before mumbling *fucking bitch* and charging back into Billy's service.

Arden and I continue doing the only thing we've been able to do for the last few minutes—stand completely still. How much time has gone by? The service is still in progress, and it must be a riveting one, because not a single person poked a head out to see what all the commotion was about. Where were the sobbing elderly aunts or inevitable latecomers when you needed someone—anyone—to burst in and interrupt?

The click of the doorknob gets my attention. "Arden," I say, following her out onto the porch. She doesn't look at me or respond when I offer her a ride, but she does follow me to my truck. "Clairebeth is really out of her mind right now. Try to forget what she said. She didn't mean those things."

"I'm not going to forget, John," she answers, shaking her head as she says, "ever." I open the truck door and Arden pauses before she climbs in. "Do you think I was leading him on all these years?" She looks at me like there's only one answer, and I'd better not think twice about not telling her the truth.

"Arden," I say, taking her shoulders in my hands. "You didn't do anything wrong by being yourself. Billy fell in love with you. You didn't realize it. You didn't feel the same way. There's no crime in that."

"When someone you care about disappears from the deck of a tugboat in the middle of the night, do you think it's possible to stop thinking about all the *what ifs*?" She bites her lower lip again.

"You mean, what if you gave him a chance?"

"Yeah, I guess," Arden says softly, pushing aside the newspaper on the seat and steps up into the truck. She is somewhere else now, talking only to herself. "Was there even a chance to give? *That* would have been leading him on. I mean, more like—what if I had taken the time to listen to him, to talk to him? What if I didn't try to pretend nothing had changed? What if I told him I didn't want to lose him?" She stops short, like she's catching herself from saying something. "And now I did lose him, *really* lose him. Now there's no going back."

I look over expecting to see tears, but Arden is staring at the dashboard, shivering. "Do you want me to drop you off at home?" I ask, handing her the black nubby sweater I'd grabbed from the sofa.

She covers her shoulders with it, nodding while keeping her gaze on the dashboard. "How do you do it?" she asks, after I slam my door shut. "How do you keep going out there for weeks at a time, totally disconnected from life?"

"I am connected to life – my life. Just because it isn't life as you and most other people know it, it's still a life."

"I'm not buying that answer." She shifts to lean against the door and face me. "Haven't you ever wanted to stick around and give reality a try?"

I don't answer right away, thinking about Meredith and how much I used to look forward to sliding into bed next to her. I'd sneak into the apartment, undress quietly, slip under the cool sheets, and feel her sleeping body respond to me. It was the closest thing I'd felt to love, but even during our best moments, I knew my feelings weren't anchored in anything real, but tethered to the hope that someone could keep me afloat when I wasn't at sea.

"Now you're not talking to me?" she asks, crossing her arms and nudging my calf with her left foot.

"I've never been in love, if that's what you mean." I slide the key in the ignition.

Arden exhales. "Sorry. It's none of my business. I don't even know you, and I shouldn't be asking you questions like this. Especially today."

"You don't have to apologize. Isn't that what days like this are for—not holding back, letting down your guard to talk about things that really matter?"

She shrugs and nods as I fire up the truck. I suddenly have a flash of Arden's parents waiting for her inside. "Want me to run back in and let your parents know you're leaving?"

"No—thanks, though, but no. They were here this afternoon." She scoops her hair back into a ponytail and releases it so dark waves fall onto her shoulders. "I couldn't even bring myself to walk into the room to look at his photo sitting on top of a coffin, and that was *before* Clairebeth opened fire. How am I going to go to his funeral tomorrow?"

I can feel her drifting off into her thoughts as I shift into gear. When I get to the edge of the parking lot, I have to wait for Sam Matthews and his menagerie of dogs to shuffle past before I can turn onto First Street. People are born. People die. And good ol' Sam Matthews still shuffles on, walking his dogs through the years.

"I guess I'll spend the night out here anyway." Arden rubs her eyes with the heels of her hands, a cluster of silver bracelets clinking softly. "I can't imagine getting on that bus back to the city. Not happening."

"Good idea," I say as the truck rolls into the dusk. "Home is where you need to be right now."

Chapter Three: Arden

Sunday, May 15 & Monday, May 16, 1994

It takes a lot to catapult my mom into reality, so I know she's officially worried when she greets me with, "Arden, you look awful. Absolutely awful," as I skulk into the kitchen with a mascara-streaked face.

"I'm sure that's an understatement," I sigh, dropping my bag on the table. It feels good to be here. Even though I never looked back after bolting to the West Coast for college and having lived in the city for almost a decade, it's hard to believe anywhere could feel more like home than this house.

"Thought about staying here tonight?" she asks, brushing the hair out of my eyes.

I nod, peeking into the living room to size up the couch before deciding my bed will be the best place to collapse. "I'm making a cocktail and calling it day."

"Maybe some warm milk instead? A drink will keep you awake."

"Right now, vodka doesn't have a chance of coming between me and sleep." I look at the clock and imagine people filtering out of the funeral home into the cool May air, leaving behind an empty room full of everything Billy.

Mom decides not to argue with me and goes into the living room to grab a rocks glass and vodka from the bar. I hear her whisper to Daddy and know he must be stretched out in front of a game. We haven't spoken since he and Mom got back from the afternoon visiting hours, and I know the Yankee game is his vodka on the rocks. Neither one of us can deal with the other being upset. I don't expect him to get up, and he doesn't want me to come in. Over the year's we've had an unspoken agreement to steer clear of each other until equilibrium is restored. We might need to come up with another game plan this time, though, since I can't imagine ever regaining my balance after losing Billy.

Mom brushes by me with her hands full, and I hear the refrigerator icemaker clink out the foundation for my drink. As she hands me the glass and puts the vodka on the kitchen table, the memory of refilling half-drained bottles with water at the end of afterschool happy hours surfaces and submerges.

"I'm going to play piano for awhile, and your father's watching the game," she says, kissing my forehead and walking into the study. Within seconds, I'm filling my glass as she fills the house with Debussy's passionate ramblings.

I climb the narrow staircase and make it to my room without turning on a single light. The number of footsteps between the landing and my doorway is permanently deposited in my memory bank from the countless times my friend Casey and I stumbled our way toward the twin beds on either side of my room. Casey Peretto was the classic loud "shhher," inevitably waking up my dad, who would then bang on the wall, shouting, "Everything all right, girls?" We'd shout back chipper good nights and pass out until the morning woke us with tequila-sharpened splinters of light.

As our senior year in high school began, Casey's occasional overnights evolved into her unofficially moving in. I remember how my mom held Casey's hand and listened intently as Casey told us that her dad had been arrested for breaking her mom's arm. Mrs. Peretto had dropped the charges almost immediately, claiming she'd been drunk too, and the details were too fuzzy.

Casey and I were drinking too enthusiastically to worry about ruined lives by the time that October rolled around. We did Cuervo shots in the parking lot before school, dove into a liquid lunch, and then chased the day with whatever we could find. I told myself I was too good a friend to let her drink alone, and the clink of our empty bottles under the seats of her gray Sapporo became a regular backbeat to our endless route—7-Eleven, Gull Pond, Clark's Beach, repeat.

I didn't know why Casey attached herself to me. She had lots of other friends. Maybe she liked me because I didn't ask her any questions; maybe she hated me because I didn't ask her any questions—my seeming ambivalence and our mutual love of tequila the only things she could really count on.

In fact, I had been constantly terrified for her, and I couldn't imagine what she was going through. Even though my parents have abrasive moments, there's a layer of something that protects them from digging into each other's Achilles' heels. That something was nameless to me when I lived at home, but now I'd call it respect.

As Casey and I settled into being temporary sisters, my life got blurrier. We traveled the road to graduation with gusto, shotgunning Budweiser tallboys and perfecting the art of the crab-claw Bloody Mary. We smoked mescal worms that had been zapped dry in the microwave, chopped up, and expertly rolled, the ensuing buzz jumpstarted by our "finish a bottle to get the worm" rule—no fishing allowed.

Once, I caught a glimpse of Casey watching my dad wrap his arms around my mom for a quick hug before he left for work. The tender moment made Casey wince like she'd banged into something sharp, but there was this glint of something else there too—a wish?

I shake off the image of that moment before it leads me to graduation morning. How many times have I lingered over a well-stowed memory not realizing that I'm opening a door, inviting it to morph into an avalanche of emotion? Not tonight. I'm in no condition to root around in the gardens of my past, digging up dirt. I close my eyes and try to zone out. The vodka is bland, cold, and good.

It doesn't take long for my thoughts to drift back to how effortless it had been to be myself around John. Even in the midst of Clairebeth's tirade, I'd felt safe knowing that he was close by.

Still, no matter what John or anyone else may say, I *do* feel like I'd been leading Billy on for years. Clairebeth hadn't been wrong about that.

I drift back to imagining John's life at sea, the same kind of dangerous, disjointed life that consumed Billy. Why is John forty and still alone? What is he hiding from?

* * *

I must have dozed off in the midst of deconstructing tugboat captains because I'm still in Sunday night's clothes when a door slapping shut wakes me. "Morning," I say aloud to no one, knowing it's time for a sail when that one word escalates into a full-blown *morning/mourning* homonym headache.

Andromeda is moored behind the house, waiting for me. Sometimes when I sit in my windowless Manhattan office, I stare at photos of gliding, keeling sailboats and imagine her bobbing on Stirling Creek.

In true "Arden's home" fashion, Mom has orchestrated a breakfast extravaganza and forces me to make a pit stop. Before she can plop down a second plate of blueberry pancakes, I stand up to give her freckled cheek a kiss. "I'll be back," I whisper in my worst Schwarzenegger.

"First swim of the season this afternoon. You should join us," she says, filling the sink with sudsy water. "Are you heading out alone?"

"Just me and *Andromeda*." I push open the door as she calls out her usual, "Careful out there!"

The closer I get to the water, the better I feel about my decision to circle the bay instead of go to Billy's funeral. I want to feel close to him, and I can't bear the thought of being around other people, especially Clairebeth.

Halfway down the dirt path, I turn toward the crunch of footsteps behind me. *John.* "Hey, Arden," he says, as if I'm expecting him. "Stopped by to see how you're doing."

"I'll be much better once I'm out on the water." I spin around and keep walking. Rude, maybe, but what is he doing just dropping by to check on me? I notice that he looks much taller, and his hair is different, a mass of inky curls that must have been tamed yesterday, though I can't imagine a tugboat captain using gel.

And then there are his eyes. Not wanting to stare, I think about all the "green" words I know, doubting that even an unabridged thesaurus would be able to deliver an exact description. Mossy sage? Too soft. Muted chartreuse? Closer. They're a luminous green, and all the more striking because his face has the ruddy complexion only seamen boast this early in the season, a sun-and-wind-induced radiance.

"I'm worried about you," John says, seemingly unaware of my scrutiny. "You're pretty damn hard on yourself. Anyone ever tell you that?"

"Billy," I answer. "All the time."

"I'm not surprised. His middle name was 'Tell it like it is.'" I can see that he's giving *Andromeda* the once over. "Want some company?"

"I kind of want to be alone . . ."

"But, you appreciate the extra set of highly-skilled hands, am I right?"

I know John is just trying to make conversation or lighten the mood or just . . . trying. "Mm, right. I imagine this sail as a tribute to Billy. So, I guess . . . yeah, why don't you come along?"

"What's her name?" John asks as he hops aboard and starts to help me with the rigging.

"*Andromeda*. It's always reassured me that Princess Andromeda was rescued from being devoured by a terrible sea monster."

"So you're into stars?"

"No, Greek mythology, though. You?"

"Obsessed. I can steer by them."

"Really?" I ask, pushing off to launch our initial glide past Alice's Fish Market and into Stirling Harbor.

"Really. For me, it's comforting to know that if I can see stars, I can find my way. There's all this order within apparent chaos. Everything has its place."

We float by Townsend Manor into a watery field of mostly occupied moorings. The morning is still unfolding, and we're one of the few boats under way.

"Billy always wanted me to ditch *rag-bagging* and go out on his boat instead," I say. "He couldn't stand being dependent on Mother Nature for power." I motion for John to flip open the small blue-and-white cooler, and his face doesn't betray any *Now? Really?* sentiments. He fishes a Heineken out of the ice and pops off the top with the opener attached to the cooler handle. I decide against explaining that the cooler wasn't packed for a 9 a.m. style but abandoned the other night after I discovered an untouched fifth in the console.

"I witnessed Billy's need for speed firsthand," he says, passing me the bottle and nodding when I hold it up and tip it toward him before taking a sip. "He could never get where he was going fast enough on a tug."

"Did you know Billy took sailing lessons?" I ask. John shakes his head. "We were eight or so, and Billy was bored on day one. They started with knots, and he already knew how to tie them all with his eyes closed." I pause, remembering something for the first time in years, maybe ever. "In fact, I think he actually reminded our teacher how to tie a bowline."

"Why am I not surprised? Did Young Billy ever learn to sail?"

"No, his grandmother died during the first week of lessons, and he spent the rest of the summer upstate with his mom's family. You know how much Billy despises lakes. I mean, despised lakes." I pause and bite down on my lip like it's the verb that jolted me. "*Shit.*" I glance over at John, but he's averting his eyes, trying to afford me the only kind of privacy two people can give each other on the deck of a small boat.

An osprey swoops overhead, scanning the water. "I can never get enough of watching them, their focus," I say, "and did you know that an osprey can turn a fish in its talons to stay aerodynamic no matter how big the catch? Not even the mighty eagle can do that."

"Impressive. I'm glad they're making a comeback." John holds up his right hand to shield his eyes from the sun. "Not that I can blame them for wanting to get the hell out of here."

"Agreed," I say, taking a long swallow of beer. "It wasn't pesticides that drove me away, but I did have my own list of reasons for wanting to leave Greenport without looking back."

"A common affliction, that insidious get-out-of-Greenport-itis," he says. "I was packed and ready to head out the day I graduated. Both feet out the door."

"Where'd you go?" I ask, still watching the osprey dip and twirl. We're past the breakwater now, and *Andromeda* cuts smoothly through the light chop as we head east on Peconic Bay.

"Where didn't I go—that would be an easier question to answer," he says, taking the tiller from me to fully catch the shifting wind. "I studied marine biology at URI, and I played with a couple of bands. Every summer, I'd go on a solo cross-country tour."

"A *tour?*"

"Yes, a *tour,*" he repeats with a *sheesh* expression. "I'd pick a route, drive all day, and then stop at bars and coffeehouses whenever I was ready to take a break from the highway. I always found a place to play, and most of the time I even made a little money too."

"You played the guitar?"

"I *still* play the guitar. And sing the songs I write."

"Is that so? I've never had a singer-songwriter on board before. Would you . . ." I stop short of making a request.

"Would I sing right now?" he asks with a grin. "Is this some kind of test?"

"I don't doubt you. I'm just curious. Billy never mentioned your musical prowess."

John doesn't respond right away. He turns his face to the wind, looking behind us as we move quietly through the water for several minutes.

"Billy was my biggest fan, and he always pushed me to really dig into my music," John says, turning back toward me.

"How did you go from college and summer tours to being a tugboat captain?"

"The summer after graduation, I got a job as a fishery reporting aide."

"Sounds very official."

"Yeah. More like officially the experience I needed to realize I wanted to do something else. I worked out of Shinnecock Canal, gathering data about tuna from recreational fisherman."

"Are you the ones who slapped them with fines for bringing in undersized fish?"

"No, I mean, we could have, yes, but that was pretty self-regulating. No one wants to be on the dock with a teeny-tiny tuna. There's a whole lotta ego there. I was asking questions, filling out forms. Somehow I'd envisioned something very different after hearing about my friend's life on Jekyll Island.

"That's off South Carolina, right?"

"Georgia. He loved turtles and got a job counting them. He made his long days on the beach and long nights with gorgeous tourists sound like a fairy tale career."

"Don't tell me Georgia trumps the Hamptons when it comes to gorgeous tourists. I won't believe you."

"I did actually have a gorgeous boss. She looked like Christie Brinkley with strawberry blonde hair, and she had this amazing . . ." He stops himself, glancing over at me.

"Don't tell me, inappropriate but worth-it summer romance?"

"I wish.More like inappropriate but worth-it summer fantasies," he laughs. "Anyway, there was something about the whole thing that just wasn't for me, not just with that job, but with where I knew I'd end up if I followed that path."

"So you went back to touring?"

"No, no, I couldn't imagine myself making an actual living from my music. I never thought of myself as someone who lacked self-esteem, but I guess I did back then, especially when it came to stuff that really mattered to me. Anyway, I knew I needed to find some kind of *real* job but decided to make a little cash to stash away first. You know, fill up my empty back account enough to give me a cushion for the job search ahead."

"Working on a tugboat was your cash cow?"

John nods. "A tugboat captain on the brink of retirement sat next to me at the Cinnamon Tree bar and helped me talk myself into becoming a deckhand. I told myself and everyone else it was the ideal job for a songwriter, since I'd have time on the boat to write and then at least two weeks off between hitches."

"Sounds ideal." We're approaching Bug Light. In 1963, the original lighthouse was destroyed by arson, and the community had rallied to rebuild it four years ago.

Morning has turned up the volume on all the colors, and it feels like Bug Light is showing off for us with its bright, white clapboard gleaming against a pearl blue sky. I love getting as close as possible and imagining what it would be like to live there.

"I guess it may have been just a little too ideal," John says. "I really liked being on the tug, and I was a natural. There's something about the rhythm of it all that suits me. It's hard to explain. More than fifteen years have gone by, and I haven't stopped towing."

"You don't sing anymore?"

"I sing all the time, but I don't play out anymore. My shows are more . . ." he laughs softly, "*contained*."

"Meaning?"

"I perform in harbors." We look at each other before coming about to point *Andromeda* toward home.

"Like in New York Harbor?" I ask. He nods. "How does that work?" I imagine John paddling around the Hudson in a kayak, serenading the seagulls.

"Can you keep a secret?"

"Not really," I admit. "It's not my strong suit. I *try* to keep secrets, but somehow they always find a way to slip out."

"Well, at least you're honest, but honesty isn't enough. I need your pledge of silence."

"OK, OK," I say, bringing my hand up to mimic zipping my lips shut. "You have my word."

"All right. I'll trust you." He sighs. "So, when I'm on the tug, I perform over the radio from the wheelhouse."

"While you're under way?" I ask. "Aren't you supposed to keep your eyes on the road, or the ocean? You know what I mean."

"I do know, and no, I'm not driving the tug and tuning my guitar at the same time. I perform when we're laying at anchor, waiting on a berth for our next orders."

"How'd you come up with that one?" I picture John gazing over gauges and charts to stare at the harbor, a guitar resting across his lap.

"It started one night when I just couldn't take the *so close and yet so far* feeling any longer. I couldn't stop thinking about the last time I'd called my girlfriend and heard an ice cream truck drive by in the background. It made my mind reel. That warped "Pop Goes the Weasel" was a jolt of reality that life was going on without me."

"Were you far from home the first time?"

"No, that's the crazy part. I was in New York Harbor, and I've gotta say, the hours I spend there can be the hardest. Home is *so close*, but I might as well be in Antarctica. That's how far away it feels."

"Can't you dock the tug and have someone call you when they need you?"

"That would be a no. The tugboat industry would've fallen flat on its ass years ago if companies allowed seamen to go ashore between tows. We float, and we wait. We wait, and we float."

"And in your case, you wait, and you float, and you sing," I say, waving to my Atlantic Street neighbors as they motor by in their Boston Whaler.

"That's right," John says. "So, I have a live radio show called the Wheelhouse Café. As far as I know, Billy and a guy I work with are the only two people who know it's me on the air."

"Why the big secret? Voice that bad?"

"It has more to do with legalities. I get on the radio and announce I'll be broadcasting from a certain channel. Then I tie off my handheld mic with a rubber band so it stays engaged and hang it from the spotlight handle."

"And then?"

"Then I sing into it."

"So, you're sitting in the wheelhouse, playing the guitar and singing? Who's listening?" I can see the breakwater in the distance. Almost home.

"I have no idea," John admits. "Could be no one, though I was at the Ear once and overheard two guys toasting that crazy fucker in the Wheelhouse Café."

"So you keep it a secret because . . ."

"Because tying up a marine radio channel is against the law."

"You really live life on the edge, don't you?" I ask, raising my eyebrows as I bump his shoulder with my fist.

We sail on in silence for a while, and I like that we can talk and then not. Billy is on my mind as I stare at Shelter Island. In third grade, our parents started letting us ride the ferry alone. We strutted on board, radiating independence. Each of us held a glass bottle with a message stuffed inside. When the ferry got to the middle of the bay, we closed our eyes and chucked our bottles overboard. For years, we had an ongoing back and forth about where all those bottles might have ended up—New Zealand, Antarctica, California—and Billy's dad would have us flip through paper-thin encyclopedia pages to learn about each destination we imagined.

"How did Billy find out it was you?" I ask. *Andromeda* glides into the creek near a small but impressively noisy flock of terns descending on the spit of beach on our starboard side.

"There was a night I knew he'd be in New York Harbor too, so I told him when to tune in. After that, Billy was a regular. It was actually great to know someone was listening." I imagine John's voice floating through the darkness to reach legions of seamen cradling hot cups of coffee while they dream of all the places they'd rather be.

"Of course, Billy had bigger plans for me," John says. "He wanted me to *do* something with my music. Make something happen."

"Like what? Get a record deal?"

"Record deal, tour, everything. He thought I was wasting my time on the tug."

I smile, remembering how Billy always wanted the biggest and best for the people he cared about. You liked running three miles a couple times a week? Train for a marathon! You made a mean cupcake? Start a bakery! In love with a girl you grew up with? Buy her a pearl bracelet and lay your heart on the floor so she can stomp all over it.

I wish I could erase the memory of that shadow covering Billy's face on my birthday. All I could do was stare at the bracelet and listen to his quiet breathing. I know the courage he had to summon to open that door, and still I only wanted him to close it so we could pretend nothing had changed.

"Do *you* think you're wasting your time?" I ask.

"I think I do what I do for a reason. Billy called that reason *fear of success*. Now I think it's all beside the point. I mean, I'm almost forty. No one's launching a musical career at forty."

"I think I have to side with Billy on this one. A musical career at forty? Why not? Maybe you won't end up playing to sold-out stadiums, but why the hell not go for it? Our limitations only exist because we let them. Sometimes we need to get out of our own way."

"You're starting to sound like an inspirational poster. Now I really see how alike you and Billy are. Must be something anchored in your preschool's philosophy."

"We're both optimists," I say, as we glide into the slip. "I guess I still am."

John hops off to grab the lines. "You know, about Clairebeth," he begins, "I hope you'll . . ."

"We don't need to talk about Clairebeth," I say, feeling less optimistic than I did a few seconds before. "I get where she's coming from. I really don't want to dwell on what happened. It makes me feel ill when I replay it in my mind."

I step off the dock and catch the sound of "Amazing Grace." It's Mom on the piano, and she's playing the song I most and least want to hear because it never fails to make me feel like I need saving.

John stands motionless next to me, listening. I know that even though crying in front of other people is on my "I never" list, it would be impossible to stop the tears that are already flowing as John sings, "How precious did that Grace appear the hour I first believed . . ."

At first, his voice is so soft I think I might be imagining it. I decide to close my eyes and hum along anyway, no longer caring how it came to be.

"Thank you," I whisper as John lifts each word into the air.

Chapter Four: John

Monday, May 16, 1994

Leaving Arden isn't easy. Sailing with her had made me feel more ... I don't know, I guess it just made me *feel*. She's so at ease on the water, and sailing gave us something tangible and familiar to focus on.

As Arden brought *Andromeda* to the dock, "Amazing Grace" was drifting down from her house, and I started singing along as I wrapped the bowline around a pile and made it fast. That's when I noticed the tears chasing each other down Arden's cheeks. I wanted to wrap my arms around her but decided to keep singing and stay busy with the boat instead. When I finished all the verses I could remember, Arden lifted her head to say, "Ever notice there's never a box of tissues around when you really need one?"

We'd both smiled as she wiped her nose with a balled-up sweatshirt, and then we walked back toward the house side by side but not touching. Before Arden stepped inside the porch door, she rubbed my arm and gave it a squeeze. From behind the screen, her shadowed face said, "'Bye, Captain John Raymond. Thanks," and then she was gone.

My first plan of action had been to head right back to the city, but then I decided to wait since I hadn't logged any Aunt Suebee time yet. I know she doesn't have a lot of company, and I want to be sure she's holding her own. I know she'd be angry to hear me say, "Suebee has her good days and her bad days," but it's the truth. On her bad days, her tangents take detours no one could follow, and sometimes she forgets what she said at the beginning of a sentence before she gets to the end. Then there are her good days, when she zooms off in convertibles while her lame nephew eats freezer-burned pizza on the porch.

Suebee is fishing some envelopes out of her mailbox when I park my truck in front of her house. I know she's a die-hard proponent of minding your own business, so she probably won't ask why I'm wearing jeans and a T-shirt instead of the suit for the funeral she'd hung on the back of the closet door upstairs.

She grins as I walk over and plop down in the wooden Adirondack chair I built for her in some long-ago shop class. This is our usual hangout. I usually read the paper while Suebee digs into a crossword. She realized long ago that I'm no secret weapon on the puzzle front. "What's an eight-letter letter word for *impartial?*" Silence. "Thanks, John."

I remember a lifetime of Easter breakfasts with forty people crammed into small, smoke-filled rooms, laughing, drinking, and making each other crazy. Exactly when had our huge family dwindled down to the two of us sitting on Suebee's front porch?

"So," she asks, taking my hand, "how are you holding up, Young John? We didn't get to talk after the wake last night." Suebee calls me Young John and my dad Old John, to his chagrin.

I tell her I'm sad, aware of how inadequate the word sounds. "It was a really heavy night. Lots of people showed up. Packed."

"Nothing worse than an empty funeral parlor," Suebee says, closing her eyes and leaning back to rest her head. "Give away free candy or better yet, money, at mine, will you? I want to make sure I pack 'em in there." Her smile makes me smile.

"His sister is really a wreck. Clairebeth's relied on him for so long."

"We all find ways of going on. Most of us, anyway. Clairebeth's young. And spunky, from what I recall. There'll always be a hole there, but she'll find her way."

"She lashed out at Arden McHale, one of Billy's old friends. Remember her?"

"Oh, sure, I see her parents from time to time. She lives in the city now, right?"

"Yeah," I say, "and Clairebeth laid into her with some really ugly accusations. It was intense."

"I hope Arden remembers Clairebeth isn't herself right now. Everyone's in an altered state when they lose someone they love. And for some, those waves of anger and sadness and regret are just too much to feel, so they find someone or something to attach them to."

"How old are you, Aunt Suebee?"

"Didn't your mother teach you to never . . ."

"Of course, of course," I interrupt. "But you're my Aunt Suebee. It's between us."

"Sorry, Charlie," she laughs. "That's between me and me."

"What if I guess?"

"What do you care?"

"I was just thinking about how cool you are, and about everything you've seen."

"I worked at the furniture store when I was in my twenties, and it was like having a window into other people's lives. I loved it. Customers would talk to each other like we weren't there. And then turn around and talk to *us* pretending to be the people they aspired to be, instead of the ones we just saw fighting and picking away at each other. Not everyone was like that, but through the years we had quite a parade of the mildly miserable and majorly disappointed."

"Is that where you met Uncle Bruce, at the store?"

"Your Uncle Bruce and I met right on this porch. He caught a glimpse of me at The Coronet, asked around for my name, and then found out where I lived. He walked right up these steps with a jar full of beach glass. Smart man. If he'd given me flowers instead, I wouldn't have given *him* the time of day."

"Bouquet overload, huh?" I ask, squeezing her hand.

"More like being weary from an overall lack of originality. I believed I was supposed to be living a different life someplace else, not working at a furniture store in Greenport. When I met Bruce, that all changed."

I stare at the steps and picture Bruce loping up them with a wry grin, presenting Suebee with sea glass. "It hasn't happened for you yet, has it?" she asks.

"You're right, a strapping young man has yet to bring me a jar of beach glass."

"It will happen," she says, ignoring my jokey response. "You're a good man with a good head on your shoulders. And you're easy on the eyes. You've just got to open yourself up to the idea that sharing your life with someone—the right someone—is infinitely better than being alone."

"I don't feel alone. I chose this life. I really don't feel like I'm missing anything."

"Sometimes you don't know what you're missing until someone shows up, and then it's like a light's been turned on, and you can't believe you were stumbling around in the dark for so long."

"How old were you when Uncle Bruce came along?"

"Twenty."

"I'm almost forty, Aunt Suebee. Love just may not be in my cards."

"I know how old you are. You're ready for love when you're ready for love. You can't make it appear on your doorstep, that's for sure." She turns to face me, holding my gaze. "But you can't keep the door locked, either. And don't think it was so obvious with your Uncle Bruce. I never considered myself a romantic, but I'd imagined . . . I don't know, a grand, explosive beginning."

"No fireworks?"

"Bruce and I definitely didn't start off with a bang. Not to mention, he'd taken my cousin from Mattituck on a date or two. When he introduced himself, I remembered his name and thought, *This boy is crazy if he thinks I'll give him the time of day after he's been chasing Josephine all over the North Fork.*"

"How'd he get you to change your mind?"

"Persistence. He didn't stop giving me a chance to see the kind of person he was. And I found out right away that Josephine and Bruce hadn't been an item after all. He took her to the movies a couple of times, but neither one was really interested in the other. She was a little annoyed with me at first, but it was a short-lived, competitive thing. Imagine— someone choosing *me* over the Strawberry Queen?"

"I just want you to know I'm not sad or lonely or pining away for someone or something I don't have. I'm a tugboat captain for God's sake," I say with dramatic flourish. "My love is the sea!" I give Suebee an eyebrow pump.

She pats my hand before we both look up to check out the noisy group of people walking down the middle of Fifth Street.

"Hello, Carla!" Aunt Suebee calls out, sliding forward to the edge of her seat. "Where you headed?"

"First swim of the season, Suebee. Join us!" It's Arden's mother, flanked by four people I don't recognize.

"No can do and no thank you, but I must say I'm impressed you're still jumping in before Memorial Day."

"It's a tradition! And you know I need to make summer last as long as possible, though I'm sure this cold spring hasn't done much to make the bay bearable." Carla looks over at me. "How 'bout you?"

I am definitely more consumed by wondering whether or not Arden is still around than how cold the still-frigid bay will feel when I blurt out, "I'll meet you down there," as Carla and company continue their bayward stroll.

"That's the spirit!" Suebee says, slapping me on the back. "Go represent the family, Young John."

I walk down to my truck and swing open the door to fish out the pair of cutoffs I keep stashed behind the seat. When I pick my head up, I see Arden skip-running around the corner of Clark Street toward the swimming posse.

A few minutes later, I arrive at Fifth Street Beach to find six insane people lined up at the water's edge. "Come on, John!" Arden shouts. "We've been waiting for you!" She's slipping on a Farmer John wet suit.

"A wet suit? That's cheating!" I shake my head, tsk-tsking with my index fingers.

"Here, here!" concurs a bare-chested man in lobster-print swim trunks whose teeth are already chattering.

Arden crinkles up her forehead. "Nothing like a rookie trying to make up new rules. I always wear this over my bathing suit. It's a tradition," she says.

"If you're gonna swim, you gotta summon up some courage," I state matter-of-factly before pulling my sweatshirt over my head. I take two large strides into the water and dive under. Instantly numb, I break the surface and spin around to face the crowd. "Let the games begin!" I yell, falling backward into the water as I beckon them with both hands.

When I pop back up, I'm surrounded by whoops of fear and delight. There's spray everywhere. Arden is on the beach, unzipping her wet suit to pull it down over her shoulders and peel it over her hips. Her emerald green tank suit would be unremarkable on most women, but Arden shimmers as she moves her curvy, muscular body toward the long dock with the self-confidence of an athlete.

She takes a big step up onto the first wooden plank and sprints to the end. I hear the thump, thump of Arden's feet and then "Whoo!" as she becomes a glimmer of green, hovering over the bay for an instant before landing with an exuberant splash.

When Arden surfaces, a momentary hummingbird transformed into a mermaid, I watch her paddle furiously toward the beach. I may be the rookie, but no one has to tell me the first swim of the season is all about getting in, not staying in.

I don't realize that I'm towel-less until I climb out of the water. My lobster trunks ally mumbles, "Forgetcha towel, son? That's what I'd call a bummer. With a capital B."

"Nice," I say. "Real nice. Thanks."

Arden's mom comes to my rescue. "I always bring extras. You can never be warm enough after that jolt." She hands me a sun-warmed blue towel.

"This is one of the best things I've done in a long time," I say, dragging the towel back and forth across my shoulders.

"You need to get out more," Arden wraps her dark waves up in coral terry cloth. Now I can really see her eyes, gray-blue kaleidoscopes reflecting the afternoon light. "You know, I'm only here because Mom's the designated ringleader, and she wouldn't leave the house without me. I've been sobbing non-stop since you and I got back from our sail, and she hasn't seen me cry since I was in junior high."

I reach out to touch her shoulder. "I am so sorry, Arden. I know this hurts."

"That it does," she sighs, "and I think I'm actually going to start crying again right now. Geez." She presses her hands to her eyes. "Hey, um, my parents are having a BBQ tonight. Come by?"

"I have to get back to the city."

"Rain check. Gotcha." Arden bends over to shove her wetsuit into a mesh bag, so I can't read her face to see if she's ambivalent about my answer or her expression holds a trace of disappointment.

"Rain check," I echo, wondering if my default answer to getting close will ever be anything other than no.

Chapter Five: Arden

Tuesday, May 17, 1994

My body might be back at work, but the rest of me? Still missing in action. The office has always been my oasis, but not today. Today, I'm feeling trapped in the one place I'd used to focus on anything and everything except for my own life.

"Arden," Shelly barks, leaning against my door with the back of her right palm resting against her forehead melodramatically. "Popsicle mailer copy . . . help! I'm jammed up." Shelly reminds me of an oversized Pippi Longstocking sans braids, all arms, legs, and red hair.

"Today?"

"I'm thinking more like . . . *now.*"

"What do you think I am, a machine?"

"You wouldn't want it any other way." Shelly gestures toward the conference room with a hitcher's thumb as she backs into the hall. She peeks around my doorway once more. "You OK? I've been thinking about you." I nod without giving her a glimpse of anything else. "All righty, then," she says, "moving on. I need you! See you in five."

Why wouldn't Shelly still think I'm *that* Arden—the person who can flip a switch to make ideas light up when deadlines loom large? That reputation got me promoted to VP just six months after I was hired, and it didn't take much longer for me to be running the company's arts and entertainment division. I can admit that I'm addicted to the constant barrage of challenges, not to mention the rush I feel trying to stay three steps ahead of what our clients need.

But losing Billy has clearly short-circuited any semblance of my former self. The fact that I'm still suffering from a dream hangover isn't helping. I conked out on the early bus back into the city, and my twisted dream was intensified by motion sickness and stale air. In it, Billy had been sitting at a diner counter, spinning the spoon in his coffee mug.

"Billy, is it really you?" I'd asked, walking up behind him. "I thought you were gone."

"I could never leave you, Arden," he'd replied. "You know you're my girl."

That's when Billy turned to face me, but he had no face, and then somehow Billy's faceless face said, "At least, I always *thought* you were my girl."

Boom. I woke up and smacked my head against the bus window. The man next to me had seemed more annoyed than concerned, letting out a sharp breath before returning to his paper.

My thoughts have been moving in exhausting circles ever since. Sometimes I'm angry. Who the hell did Billy think he was, falling into the ocean? Sometimes I'm happy. Remember all the times Billy had to jump out of my parents' car while I downshifted into second gear because I was afraid I'd never find first again if I came to a complete stop? Sometimes I'm terrified. What was going through his mind when he was swallowed by the waves? Most of the time I'm just sad. How will I ever get used to the fact that Billy is gone?

And then, there's John. My imagination has produced a grainy, sepia video of him singing "Amazing Grace" in a tugboat wheelhouse. I keep playing it over and over again in my mind, and it becomes a fleeting but welcome break from the heaviness stifling me.

I hear footsteps outside my office door and know Shelly is back on her direct mail mission. "I'll meet you in the conference room," I say as she creeps by waving a piece of paper with "Help!" scrawled across it.

My phone rings as I stand up. "This is Arden."

"This is Chase aka Tucker. How are you, Arden? I've been worried about you."

Tucker. I simultaneously wince and smile at the nickname I gave Chase after our first date, when he'd tucked a very intoxicated me into bed and left me to sleep it off after making sure I downed a glass of water and Tylenol.

"Just got back. I needed an extra day to get my bearings, or at least try to." I hadn't even thought to call Chase to let him know what was happening. In fact, I hadn't thought about him at all while I was in Greenport.

"I'm sure you're exhausted." His voice doesn't sound anything other than concerned.

"I am. It's all kind of a blur. I got to the wake a few minutes after Billy's sister had started talking, so I stayed in one of the side rooms. You know, I never even made it in to talk to his parents." *What had I been thinking?* This is the first time it dawns on me that I never paid my respects to Billy's parents. Did they wonder why I didn't show up?

Chase can tell I'm distracted. "Listen. His parents will understand. You can call them. Or stop by next time you're out. They'll appreciate that even more than you being at the service. I remember when my cousin died; there was this frenzy in the beginning, and then . . ." I appreciate that he stops his make-Arden-feel better story midsentence.

"Yeah, so . . . yeah, I'll definitely reach out to them. I just can't believe that I didn't . . . I mean, God, I didn't even sign the book. Not that I care that there's no *record* of me being there when I was technically there but not *there*, but it does bother me that I totally zoned out on seeing his parents."

"It's OK, Arden. Let it go," Chase says. "There's no easy way to process all this. Hey, you know I'm around if you want to talk through anything."

"Could you meet me today—like now?" I ask, pulling the idea of escape out of nowhere. "I could use some fresh air."

There's barely a beat between my invitation and his reply. "I think that could be arranged."

"How about Mulvaney's in twenty?" I suggest, a little surprised that Chase is willing to drop out of his day to meet me.

"If Mulvaney's is your idea of fresh air, who am I to argue?" he kids. It's always dusk at Mulvaney's, and this day demands a dimmer switch.

I make an unsuccessful attempt at a swift exit, popping into the conference room to tell Shelly our brainstorm is on the back burner. "Where you going, Arden?" she asks, and I can tell she's no longer in Popsicle mode. "I'm really worried. You look so out of it."

I exhale aloud and strum my fingers on the conference room table. "I'm having a pretty tough time, so I'm going to meet a friend at Mulvaney's."

"You're meeting someone at *our* place, Arden? Have you no shame?" Shelly opens her eyes wide in mock horror. "Well, at least tell me who he is . . . give me that much, will you?"

"You don't know him. *I* barely know him." Was it possible that my first "date date" with Chase had only been a couple of weeks ago? So much has happened since we decided to walk beyond the diner to have drinks and dinner at Lefty's.

"Does this lucky stranger have a name?" Shelly asks. I know her tricks all too well and appreciate her obvious attempt to bolster my mood with a distraction.

"His name is Chase. And, lucky Chase even has a nickname, since he was unlucky enough to be with me when I broke my number-one rule pertaining to drinking tequila shots on a first date."

"And that would be . . ."

"Don't drink tequila shots on a first date." Shelly snort laughs aloud several times as I tell her about table dancing, my Chase-supported stumble home, and the late night tuck-in. Then she gives me a squeeze and shoos me out of the conference room. I'm cleared for takeoff.

When I get to Mulvaney's, Chase is already waiting inside, and I wonder how he managed to get there before me. "Cocktail or coffee?" he asks, as I slide into the booth.

"Both," I reply, already relaxing. Everything waits patiently at Mulvaney's. Back in high school, Casey probably would have called it *lurking on the fringes*, but to me it's more comforting than that, like there's a permanent no-rushing policy in effect. During the few months Casey had lived with us, she and I took countless field trips in search of places like this, pubs and dive bars where problems get dim and "What'll it be?" is the only question that needs answering.

"Both it is, then," Chase says, interrupting my memory.

A waitress with a Tweety Bird tattoo perched on her left breast realizes she has company. "What can I get for you?" she asks Chase, leaning toward him without acknowledging my presence.

"I'll have an Absolut martini with two olives," I jump in, "dirty. And a double espresso." I've experienced what I call "The Chase Effect" since the first time we shared a plate of cheese fries at the diner. In his orbit, women of all ages, shapes, and sizes spin into an alternate universe. The fact that Chase seems oblivious to their spiraling only fuels their fascination . . . that, and how he personifies an irresistible oxymoron—buttoned-up surfer. With his tousled, sandy curls and an upper body cut into a broad-shoulder, narrow-waist triangle, he even stands out in his Wall Street–ready dark gray suit. I am sure that beyond unhinging women passing by him on the sidewalk, Chase has been responsible for more than a few whiplash epidemics when he swims laps at the Y.

"Maker's on the rocks for me, please," he orders with a nod.

"All righty then. Got it." Tweety says, taking in the view for a few backward steps before she turns toward the bar.

"So here we are, Arden McHale—Mulvaney's at eleven on a Tuesday morning," Chase says, looking around. "I see that we're joined by the usual suspects." He throws a sideways glance toward the crew of four men holding court at the bar.

"Thanks for meeting me. I know it must be tough for you to break away."

"Only as tough as I perceive it to be." He stretches both arms overhead and then brings them down slowly to rest on the table. "I'm concerned about you," he says, leaning toward me. "Of course I'll break away from my day to be with you. That's what friends do."

"Correction. That's what a friend like you does." I roll my shoulders forward and back in an unsuccessful attempt to unkink from my morning bus ride.

"Enough already," he whispers with a wink. Tweety brusquely lines our drinks up in front of us. She's visibly annoyed at being ignored in spite of the two buttons she'd undone to reveal Sylvester crouched at the ready, doomed to reach around her breast toward his yellow nemesis for all eternity.

I think about the night I picked my cousin Garrett up from Aunt Macy's dance studio on Second Avenue and saw Chase for the first time. He was standing in the middle of the room talking to Aunt Macy when I walked in. The petite blonde woman on his arm wearing high-heeled Mary Janes and a short, flouncy skirt had clearly taken dressing for a dance lesson date seriously.

Like most of the men I've observed around Aunt Macy, Chase couldn't hide his appreciation for her exotic yet somehow approachable beauty. My freckled, fair-haired mother says Macy leapt into their father's Puerto Rican gene pool with gusto, completely eschewing their maternal Irish roots. It's true. She has a follow-these-curves-if-you-dare body, the luminous Rivera family complexion, and light chestnut eyes flecked with spring's first greens.

When Garrett and I walked by their pre-lesson powwow en route to our weekly breakfast-for-dinner date, my eight-year-old cousin had to say, "'Bye, Grandma Macy!" Not that calling her out ruffled my aunt. Even though Macy wasn't too thrilled with the idea of becoming a grandmother at thirty-eight, she wears the title proudly.

Aunt Macy had chuckled and stopped us to hug Garrett and introduce me to Chase. I remember how Chase had squeezed my hand when he shook it and then asked for my card after learning I work with lots of artists. He called me later that night to admit he wasn't really interested in art but wanted to ask if I'd consider tutoring one of my aunt's struggling students. Instead of confessing that I'm rhythmically challenged, I decided to tell him the truth—I know a lot more about tequila than I do about the tango.

Now we're poised to throw back some cocktails on an already blurry Tuesday morning. I eyeball the choices before me. "What's the old saying, 'Martini before espresso, never sicker'?"

"Something like that," Chase says, raising his rocks glass to clink against my espresso cup.

"So, I keep thinking I'm fine, and sometimes I almost believe it," I begin, hoping that talking will distract me from being distracted by the intensity of Chase's almost denim blue eyes. "Then I catch myself staring off into space and realize I've completely zoned out. There's this tight knot in my stomach that won't go away. And the past few nights, I've only scratched the surface of sleep. I wake up achy and *really* grouchy."

"You? Grouchy? I find that hard to believe." Chase takes another sip.

"What bothers me most is I don't think . . ." I pause. "I mean, I *know* I don't have a right to feel this disoriented. I took Billy for granted. Instead of being a friend, I just ignored a situation that made me uncomfortable. Maybe subconsciously I was hoping time would make things better, but I can't give myself that much credit. And now there's no time left." I tip my glass up, drinking most of the martini in one gulp. *Better.*

"You lost me there." He grabs my hand before continuing. "And you don't have to explain, I just want you to know I'm not completely following you."

"But I want to explain." I sigh. "I've told you Billy was one of my oldest friends. We met in nursery school, and until my thirtieth birthday, we were thick as thieves." I fill Chase in on the avalanche of everything that followed and then take a sip of espresso followed by a martini swig.

Chase leans in even closer, his bourbon-laced breath drawing me closer. "Hindsight is twenty-twenty. You can't believe what happened between you is the reason Billy's gone—no matter what his sister says."

"I can't ignore Clairebeth's accusations. How could I be so completely self-absorbed that I didn't notice Billy was in love with me? For years? And when he finally summons the courage to put himself out there, I'm stunned into silence. And then, I pull a classic Arden by deciding my best strategy is to pretend nothing happened. You know, let some time pass, and then everything will magically go back to normal. I'm a selfish idiot and the furthest thing from a friend that . . ."

"I have to stop you there. Blaming yourself is not bringing Billy back."

"Blaming myself is the only thing I'm capable of right now. I feel like I betrayed someone who knew me—*really* knew me—and still loved me. And when Clairebeth flipped out at the wake, every word she said sounded like the truth."

I wonder if Chase hears me inhale sharply after the word "truth," or if I'm the only one who feels like the sound ripped the room open. I'm familiar with the nuances of truth and wonder how long I'll keep on lying by omission. My editing prowess extends far beyond intern's press releases to the stories in my own life.

"If you could hit rewind and land on your birthday, what would you do this time around?"

"That's an easy one. I'd call Billy the next day and ask him to meet me for a sail. Out on the bay, I'd tell him how much he meant to me."

I can tell that something about my tone confuses Chase when he asks, "Ever wonder if there was something more between you?"

I shake my head. Steady now. "In some ways he was like a brother, but there were these moments when I'd feel a spark. I can't define it, really, and it could have just been the spark of two people connecting, not necessarily romantically or sexually, just simpatico. Now I know I loved Billy enough that maybe I should have at least opened myself up to the thought of us together. The whole thing just took me by surprise, and then I was too uncomfortable and confused to say the right thing—to say much of anything, really."

I catch Tweety's eye, holding up my empty martini glass as I feel myself getting closer to the edge of what's been gnawing at me. Could Billy have mistaken the handful of times we spent the night wrapped around each other on my bedroom floor as something more than drunken hookups?

"Was Billy out on the tugboat a lot?" Chase asks, and I'm glad he's punctual and thoughtful and gorgeous but not a mind reader.

"If you call every two weeks a lot, and I do, then yes. But then when we'd see each other, talk on the phone, it'd be like we were picking up in the middle of a conversation. You know, the way it is with good friends."

"I do know. It's pretty rare, and rarer still for four-year-olds to become lifelong friends."

"Three," I say, sampling my fresh martini as soon as Tweety places it in front of me. "We met when we were three."

"Three," Chase echoes. "I stand corrected."

"This isn't very fun for you, is it?"

"Fun? No. Do I want to be anywhere else? No." He looks at me hard, like he's memorizing my face.

"Chase," I say, not taking my eyes off his.

"Yes?"

"You're making me a little self-conscious here." When his gaze doesn't shift, I continue. "It feels like I'm back in high school with someone staring down the lone zit on my forehead."

"Sorry. What can I say? You're intoxicating right now." Am I imagining things, or does the man behind The Chase Effect actually sound starry-eyed?

"On my way to being intoxicated, maybe, but intox*icating*? That's a stretch. And I think the fact that I've introduced zits into our conversation means it should end. Immediately." I want to dim the spotlight.

"Don't talk yourself out of being here, Arden." Chase is clearly ignoring my attempt to fast-forward. "It's a sad time and not one you want to linger in, but you're right here. And your eyes are bright. And every word you're saying is welling up from deep inside you. You're remarkable. Billy knew it, and I know he wouldn't want you to second-guess everything. He knew he was important to you. A momentary glitch isn't capable of erasing your history together."

I nod, staring down at the table. "When it comes to dealing with something difficult, I have a tendency to hash, rehash, and then hash once more just to be sure. But you've already figured that one out, haven't you?"

"Yeah," he says, tapping the right side of his forehead with his index finger. "Got it."

"I should probably get back to the office," I say, scanning the room for a clock, even though I know a place like Mulvaney's doesn't burden its patrons with a nuisance like time.

Chase pulls out his wallet and leaves some money on the table. "Let's go. How about I take you out for Pad Thai later on?"

"Sorry, gotta work. Gallery opening at seven. I expect to see you there, and bring a friend. Unless of course you have another salsa class and were planning to take me for Thai before you put your dancing shoes on . . ." I raise an eyebrow to rib him about his frequent classes. "Awww, Chase. Do you have a crush on my Aunt Macy? I think I just made you blush."

He shakes his head as he slides out of the booth. "I don't blush that easily. But you, senorita, should think twice before teasing me about being suave on the dance floor." He shifts his hips from left to right and reaches out for my hand.

Before grabbing it, I take a final swallow of coffee. "Caffeine, cocktails, and Chase—the remedy for what ails me."

And I have to admit; I do feel lighter in spite of myself.

Chapter Six: John

Tuesday, May 17, 1994

Believe me, I get it. I don't expect Aunt Suebee to give up hoping that I'll find love. I know she doesn't want me to die a lonely sailor, and I also know I'll never make her understand what I love about the rhythm of my life, with its days and weeks flowing like the tides.

When I'm on the boat, my life is six hours on, six hours off. The destinations change—I could be heading north to Maine or end up Savannah-bound—but what consumes my day stays pretty much the same. I'm either pushing a deep-loaded oil barge through the mayhem of New York Harbor, or I'm offshore towing, rotating my view between the barge astern, the nothingness on the horizon and the glowing specs on the radar.

When I'm off watch, I eat, sleep, and write songs. And sure, I'm no different than every other seaman, spending every waking hour wondering what the hell I'm doing at sea and if there's something better somewhere else. That's the tie that binds us.

My crew, I know them just enough. We're no different from any dysfunctional family, so I keep to myself as much as possible. When I'm at sea, silence is golden.

And while figuring out how to coexist in a confined, isolated space may not seem like rocket science, some guys just don't seem to get it. I learned how to read my first captain like a book. If Captain Les was wearing his glasses, I knew his mood was so foul that he couldn't even be bothered to put his contacts in. And if he came up during my watch and leaned against the other side of the wheelhouse with his arms crossed, glaring out the window like he was trying to stare down the sea, I kept my mouth shut. If he wanted to talk, he'd talk.

I cringed each time a clueless idiot asked Les about the one thing guaranteed to send the old man over the edge whether or not he had his glasses on—crew change. "Do I look like I have a fucking crystal ball? Maybe you should stop asking me stupid shit and start working."

Then there were captains like Tony Battani, who used their imaginations to turn the tug into whatever they wanted it to be. In Tony's case, it was a kitchen. Every Friday, he'd start making meatballs from scratch. On Sundays, our boat became a floating Italian drive-through, doling out Tony's meatballs to any tugs lucky enough to be in that harbor. And if dispatch happened to call for a job while Tony was in Chef Boyardee mode? He'd say he was busy making Sunday dinner, and if that didn't get us off the hook, he'd say we had a line in the wheel and a diver in the water.

When I'm home for two or three weeks at a stretch, an entirely different crew of crazies surrounds me. Mrs. Noonaby, who I have yet to see without a cat in her arms, lives on my starboard side. To my port, there's Charles the Mad Scientist, who wakes me with late-night explosions and foul smells instead of loud music and drunken antics.

When it comes to my perpetual bachelorhood, some women wish I could be a man who'd taken marriage for a test drive that crashed and burned instead of a someone who's never even gotten behind the wheel. My ex Meredith, on the other hand, seemed even more interested in me when she discovered I was what she referred to as "baggage-free."

Meredith and I didn't just meet at party; we literally collided reaching down to pick up a napkin. My head didn't hurt, but I felt dizzy when I looked up and was face to face with a knockout. I was so flustered that it felt like I had to remember how to talk before I could ask if she was all right, apologize, and introduce myself.

For months, our relationship was all about tumbling into her bed after a night out and not getting up until it was time to meet a crowd of her friends for brunch the next day. Brunch. That was a new one for me.

Moving in together was more an evolution than a decision. By the time her lease was up, she'd already taken over my bedroom closet and the medicine cabinet. She didn't tell me that she loved me or ask what I thought about us living together, but she did tell everyone that being in Chelsea was so much cooler than living on the Upper West Side, not to mention more convenient.

Convenient. That it was. And since I went to sea every couple of weeks, our souring relationship teetered on the edge of spoiling way beyond its actual expiration date.

I remember the feeling of relief when I got back to the boat. I was anxious to be as far away from Meredith as possible and determined to end things when I got back. That determination had a way of dissolving as soon as I'd step through our door two weeks later. It was like I had temporary amnesia and was seeing Meredith for the very first time. *What was so wrong with us anyway?*

It got easier and easier to answer that question, no matter how much time we spent apart. I'll bet that whoever said, "Absence makes the heart grow fonder," never lived with Meredith. Even though I kept switching from game over to fresh start as I went from dock to door, it didn't take long for welcome-home showers for two and mad dashes to our bedroom to be replaced with raucous fights and silent standoffs. I was always "disconnected from reality with the fucking nerve to show up like time stood still until I got off the boat," while she seemed "sneaky, demanding, and almost determined to find something fucked up between us to harp on."

The last two months with Meredith were the loneliest. My tolerance for ignoring the reality of our relationship had been whittled from threadbare to nonexistent. The moment I caught myself actually counting the hours until I got back on a tug was when I finally admitted to myself that it was over between us.

And yet, even with my newfound resolve, I was blindsided when Meredith broke up with me first. "John, I think this is the end of the line for us. You know it's not working. I know it's not working. We need to move on."

My first reaction had been anger that she'd beaten me to the punch. She'd sounded breezy and dropped the bomb while I was standing in the kitchen making a turkey sandwich, like she didn't even consider breaking off our two-year relationship worthy of a sit-down conversation.

I remember being so fucking exhausted that all I wanted to do was to move out and move on, but Meredith and I had so much to sort through before we could go our separate ways—furniture, artwork, a cat. Within a few days, I learned that Meredith had been running around with another guy for four months. It made sense; her matter-of-fact breakup spiel had seemed a bit too cool. I never wanted to believe that Meredith would fuck around on me. It was like someone really big and angry had punched me in the gut . . . hard.

Spending years at sea has given me time to discover how my mind works when I'm jammed up. After I found out about Meredith, I knew it would be too easy to let feeling like a fool trump what I was really feeling—relief. I'm still glad that I didn't know she was cheating on me until later, because I actually believed we'd understood each other in those last few moments—the loneliness, the frustration, the readiness to move on. Fuck her for having a head start.

I'd forgotten how good it felt to be at ease in my own home and then, sooner than I expected, it was if I'd landed back in my own life. During those first few post-Meredith days, Billy crafted a master "comeback" plan to keep me busy. "You're like a male Julia Roberts," he said. "Women aren't intimidated by her and want to be her friend. Men think she's hot. Ever think about *that*, Captain Raymond?"

"Can't say that I have. But as long as men don't think I'm hot, and women don't want to just be friends . . . that's cool."

"I'm sure plenty of men think you're hot, but that's not my point."

I don't really remember what Billy's point was, but I do know he stayed true to form, ignoring me as he rambled on about how I needed to get back in the game. It was hard to believe Billy wasn't around to give me any more pep talks.

* * *

My phone rings, snapping me back into the moment. "John?" the voice says. "Hi, it's Arden."

"Arden, hey." I can't possibly sound as surprised as I feel.

"Glad you showed up yesterday. It was a good thing for me to take that sail with someone else."

"It was good for me too."

"Sometimes you think you want to be alone but that's exactly what you don't need and then . . ." Arden stops short for a deep breath. "Sorry. I didn't call you for a therapy session." She lets out a quick, soft laugh. "Let me start over. Hi, John. Just calling to say it was good to go sailing together *and* to invite you to a gallery opening tonight."

"Tonight?"

"Tonight. Around seven. I know it's short notice, but I remember Billy telling me how much you like art. This painter is on the verge—pretty spectacular." Her voice is accelerating. "I'm planning and promoting the opening."

"Thanks for thinking of me," I say. "Good timing too. I don't head back out till tomorrow."

"To Greenport?"

"No," I chuckle. "Back to the other most exciting place on earth—the tug."

"For how long?"

"Two weeks. And then I'm off for two."

"Oh yeah, *that* schedule. The one where you have stretches of uninterrupted time to write the hell out of some songs."

"I guess that's one way to look at it."

"Any Wheelhouse Café shows in the works?"

"Depends."

"Vague answer. I like that. Any chance I could listen in if, in fact, you do decide to grace the harbor with your talent?"

"Depends."

"Now you're just being redundant. Depends on . . ."

"On where you live."

"I'm on the East Side—Murray Hill near the FDR."

"That's prime tugboat territory, little lady. Now, how about a VHF marine radio? Got one of those?"

"You don't make it easy, do you?" I imagine her smile widening.

"Is anything worthwhile ever really easy?" I ask.

"Ha," she replies before giving me the gallery name and address. "I'll see you tonight."

"I'll see you tonight," I echo.

As I pack espresso into a stovetop pot, I remember we hadn't exchanged numbers, so Arden actually had to make an effort track me down. Then I think about her invitation. Was it a casual *come on down to the gallery?* or more like a *we need bodies at this event to prove we're doing our job, so let me invite every person I know?* Or was it something closer to a date?

Chapter Seven: Arden

Tuesday, May 17, 1994

When I get back to the office, Shelly and I huddle in the conference room, whipping together a Popsicle strategy as she grills me about my cocktails with Chase.

"Sounds like he's pretty into you," she says.

"Seems to be, but I don't know, though . . ."

"What?" Shelly starts making *you're crazy* circles with her index fingers on both sides of her head. "Is he too *normal* for you? Do you think you could actually allow yourself to like someone who's attentive *and* hot *and* successful? God, the more I go on, the more I feel like I loser. If you recall, my last potentially romantic encounter was with a guy who wore more gold chains than I've owned in my entire life, a fact my sweet Aunt Agnes forgot to mention when she set me up on that blind date from hell."

"How could I forget? You know your next date can only be better, Shell."

"Whatever," she says, waving me off. "Stop deflecting, would you? For once, we're talking about *you* here. I know you're a wreck about Billy, but you've seemed *eh* about Chase from the very beginning."

"Do I really seem *eh?*" I ask, wondering how much closer to the beginning it was possible to be. "I mean, he's . . ."

"Enough," Shelly cut me off. "Let's not get into the minutiae. What's the bottom line?"

"I'm into him," I say firmly. "At least, I think I am."

"Ever imagine him naked?"

I perk up at that—hadn't I just been distracted by the idea of Chase at the Y? "Not naked, no, but in his bathing suit."

"Geez, Arden, way to extend taking it slow to your daydreams. But hey, at least that's progress. Let's consider it your imagination getting warmed up."

"I gotta run, Shell," I say, steering clear of the imagination comment. "This day, it is a-dwindling. I need to head over to the gallery soon."

"You have all the best accounts," Shelly says as we walk back to our offices. "There are never any Popsicle openings."

Sometimes she makes my head spin, but there's something about Shelly's Chase tirade that gives me an idea. I *have* been thinking about someone, and I decide to invite John to the gallery opening. Osla, the artist, is fascinated with the sea, and even if you don't like her work, you can't escape being affected by its energy. John will love it. And she'll probably love him too.

The rest of the afternoon is uneventful. My Type A hardwiring finally decides to surface, making it possible for me to stop thinking about Billy long enough to cross a few things off my list. It's numbing to return phone calls and sort through the stack of papers on my desk.

Around four, I look at the two outfits I keep hanging on the back of my office door—a fitted black sheath and a pull-out-all-the-stops party dress. I shimmy into the sheath, slip on high-heeled, black sandals and take a cab down to the gallery. A new intern is already inside getting everything in motion, but I have some doubts about her ability to follow directions. My boss has a stereotypical penchant for hiring interns most likely to wear short skirts and least able to actually make our lives easier. Each young woman usually lasts for about a month before things fall apart and the process starts all over again.

As I step out of the cab, I notice that any hint of early summer mugginess has dissipated, and the temperature has dipped just enough to be noticeable. I start to feel a little pre-event buzz creeping in, and the dreadful but sweet anticipation makes me crave a well-made cocktail.

When I round the corner onto 24th Street, I spot Chase bending down to talk to a small boy outside the gallery entrance. Garrett. I pick up the pace, imagining the hug in my future.

"Arden! It's you!" Garrett yells, running toward me with his arms flailing.

"Garrett! It's you!" I shout back. As he throws his arms around my neck, I breathe in the smell of his hair. He's brimming with perpetual first-day-of-summer enthusiasm. "You are the perfect surprise for this weary woman."

"You never know when I'm gonna show up on the scene, do you?" he asks, almost dancing in place. The kid never stops moving.

"I can only hope it's as often as possible. You make my day." I stand up to give Chase a peck on the cheek, wondering why he has Garrett in tow.

"Hello, Arden," Chase says, grinning. "I told Garrett this show was not to be missed, and his grandmother happily agreed that boys' night out would be more fun than having Garrett watch her tap dance lesson. So here we are."

"I'm very happy to see you both, but you do realize you're over an hour early?"

"Very aware," Chase answers. "Your team did a great job of communicating all the details. Seven to Ten. Bellinis. Hors d'oeuvres. A chance to meet the artist and mingle with people who appreciate events like this."

"Nice," I say. "So you're going to hang out here in anticipation of it all?"

"Big G wants to take his favorite cousin out for a pre-event ice cream cone," Chase says. "That would be you."

I look down to see Garrett nodding his head. "I'm a man with a plan," he says, his cocoa eyes bright.

"Best plan I've heard all day, but I have to make sure things are in shipshape here before the crowds show up."

"That's what Chase said, but I needed to hear it from the horse's mouth. Not that I think you're a horse, but you know what I mean," Garrett says, already galloping down the sidewalk. "See you soon!"

"It's all about the ice cream, isn't it?" I ask Chase.

"Go get 'em," he says, blowing me a kiss before turning to jog down the sidewalk after Garrett.

Whole lotta Chase today, I think. Why does that seem so exhausting? Maybe I should've kept my distance and not let my guard down at Mulvaney's?

Stepping into the gallery, I'm immediately relieved by the explosion of color and the hum of something about to take flight. Kendra, the intern, practically sprints over to me. "I finished all the press kits," she rattles, "and the caterer is setting up, and everyone else is doing what they're supposed to be doing."

"That's a good thing," I say, relaxing a bit. She *does* have some functioning brain cells after all.

"Do you want a Bellini?" she asks.

I nod. "Never underestimate the importance of quality control."

I know Osla won't show up until the party is well under way. She's probably still in her studio, covered in paint. Osla's not a diva looking for a grand entrance, but she does struggle with the concept of time. *Ignores* the concept of time is more like it. Sometimes I envy the way she exists on another plane entirely, a place where days of the week and clocks are tiresome tools for other people. I only allow when and where slip away when I'm on *Andromeda*, and lately I've let sailing take a backseat to meetings and projects.

A few minutes before seven, the first flock of early birds walks through the door. John is one of them. I watch him scan the room, and his face lights up when he finds me.

"Hey, Captain," I say, meeting him in the center of the room. "So glad you could come." I lean into him for a kiss on the cheek. "Flowers?"

John hands me what appears to be a haphazard bunch of wild flowers but is probably an extremely expensive, carefully planned arrangement from one of the neighborhood florists. "Flowers," he repeats. "Yes."

"For Osla?" I ask.

"Who's Osla?"

I laugh out loud. "The artist."

"Oh, no," he says. "No, they're for you."

"Wow. Thanks. I'm not used to getting flowers . . . at an opening, I mean. They're beautiful." I can tell John doesn't feel at all self-conscious about giving me the bouquet. He's already looking over my shoulder at a painting behind me.

"That's a favorite of mine," I say. "You can tell Osla was totally inside it when she painted it. Even though there are so many different colors at play, it's like her paintbrush never left the canvas."

"Makes me feel like swimming," he says.

"I'm surprised our chilly preseason dip didn't turn you off to swimming altogether."

"Why do you say that, Miss I-Want-To-Wear-A-Wetsuit?"

"I've never seen anyone's teeth chatter as much as yours did," I tease back. "You've recovered nicely."

"How're you holding up?" John's question stings, piercing the bubble of busyness where I keep trying to hide. I focus on the softness in his voice, a voice so kind and filled with concern that it coaxes me into the present.

"I'm still standing." I force myself to look into his eyes and hope he can see both my appreciation and my need to stay outside myself if I'm going to remain standing.

As he holds my gaze, another wave of people flows in. "Time to spring into action," I say. "Will you excuse me?"

"Yes, of course. I'll see you around."

The next hour breezes by with nonstop introductions and a string of fires to put out, everything from running out of ice to a *New York Times* critic almost choking on a crab cake. John circles the room, keeping to himself. He appears to be thoroughly engrossed.

Osla arrives almost ninety minutes later. She strides into the gallery holding Garrett's hand with Chase and Aunt Macy following close behind. "Sorry, Arden," Osla says. "I was shanghaied on the way over here."

"It was an ice cream conspiracy," Chase says, looking at me apologetically. "We had no idea Osla was the artist. She walked by, saw us eating ice cream, and the next thing we knew . . ."

"Eating ice cream?" Osla interrupts. "Is *that* what you call twirling and dipping a beautiful woman on the sidewalk?" She gives Aunt Macy a wink.

"It's called *salsa dancing*, Osla," Garrett says seriously, already eyeing the hors d'oeuvre table.

My twirled and dipped aunt laughs and puts her lovely arms around me. "You look exquisite," she whispers in my ear. "And this Chase, he's quite something, isn't he?" Aunt Macy is radiant. Her clingy mango wrap dress and four-inch heels make it even harder than usual to believe she's a grandmother.

I shift gears to focus on having Osla make the rounds. "Please excuse us as we go spread some artist love," I say, draping my left arm around Osla's shoulders. "You all go ahead and make yourselves at home. The guy over there in the blue shirt is John Raymond. Make that *Captain* John Raymond, my tugboat friend from Greenport." I look at Garrett with my very goofiest exaggerated eyebrow expression.

"Tugboat?!" Garrett squeals. He grabs Chase's hand to yank him toward John. Aunt Macy stays put, surveying the room. I can tell she's already made more than one man grateful he decided to come to Osla's opening. Seeing the room vibrate with conversation and creativity makes me feel grateful to be there too.

Chapter Eight: John

Tuesday, May 17, 1994

I look down to see a boy jumping around like a human pogo stick. "Hey, there," I say, squatting to his eye level. "Are you really that glad to meet me?"

"You have a tugboat?" he asks. "Can you take me for a ride?"

"Yes to the second question," I answer. "And I drive a tug. Can't say that I own one."

I stand up to shake his father's hand. "Hi, I'm John Raymond. Too bad your son's not more outgoing."

"Yeah, Garrett's always full speed ahead," he says. "I'm Chase Sommers, and Garrett is a friend of mine."

"Are you a friend of the artist?" I ask, as a woman with the shiniest hair I'd ever seen leans over to whisper something in Garrett's ear.

"I'm more like a fan of the PR maven *behind* the artist," Chase replies, looking over at Arden.

"Chase is Arden's *boyfriend*." Garrett giggles.

"Garrett," Chase shakes his head at the boy, unflustered.

First I feel off balance, like the room has been resting on a giant ball that just rolled onto its side. Then I'm annoyed with myself. I barely know Arden. Do I really care whether or not she has a boyfriend?

The woman next to Garrett steps forward to introduce herself. "I'm Macy, Arden's aunt. And I swear my grandson just moved faster than the speed of light to meet you when Arden told us you're a tugboat captain."

"How do you know Arden?" Chase asks.

"We're both from Greenport," I explain, still trying to figure out how the bombshell next to me could possibly be a grandmother. "We reconnected at the wake of a mutual friend."

"Billy," Chase says, watching Garrett walk toward the appetizer spread. "Yeah, Arden's really a mess about losing him."

"They went through a lot together," I say. "Not many people still have friends from preschool."

"Sounds to me like not many people have friends like Billy. Arden told me they'd been having a rough time, and she's still . . ." Chase stops midsentence and seems to be looking for Arden. "Yeah, it's been tough for her. I want her to stop being so hard on herself."

I'm surprised not only by how much Chase knows about Arden and Billy, but how he's laying it all out there for me. Is he trying to make sure I know that he and Arden are close? "I don't know much about their friendship," I say, having a hard time getting the words out and an even harder time letting air in. My throat feels tight. "I just know Billy was a good guy, and he cared about her . . . a lot."

"No doubt," Chase says, watching Garrett balance a plate piled high with potato chips next to a mound of dip, a lone carrot dangling from his mouth. "Well, it's good to meet you, man. I'm sure I'll see you around tonight."

I shake Chase's hand and watch him walk away. He definitely seems to have it together—tailored but understated clothes, a high-wattage smile, and the ability to effortlessly become part of Arden's world.

I wander over to a painting that reminds me of a bruised October sky. It's like Osla had taken a pair of scissors, snipped down a patch of clouds, and then squeezed thick ribbons of blue-black, choppy frosting on top of them. I want to run my fingers over the knots of color, knowing each swirl would throb with a familiar ache. Instead, I drum my fingers on my thigh and whisper the words to "Cold October Evening," a song I wrote on the first autumn night when the temperature took a nosedive, and it seemed colder than bitter February.

"Hey, John, there you are," Arden says, placing her hand on my shoulder. "This is Osla. Osla, meet my friend, John Raymond. *Captain* John Raymond."

I shake Osla's hand, holding onto it as I say, "I'm mesmerized tonight. Truly. And this one, I feel like I've been there." Osla is waiflike and seems even tinier wearing a dress that looks like layer upon layer of sheer, pastel-colored scarves.

"Really?" Osla claps, visibly pleased. "We'll have to talk about that." She gives me a blatant once-over before going on. "So nice of you be here tonight. There's nothing scarier than hanging it all and then wondering if anyone will really care anyway. Shit. Forget caring—will they even show up?"

I let go of her hand and laugh. "Well, you've got a big crowd, and they seem to be having fun. That's a good sign, isn't it?"

"It's Arden," Osla says. "She always insists on champagne because she believes it makes people happy, and happy people have an easier time parting with their money."

"We already sold two paintings." Arden is beaming. "And I'm sure we'll get a few more on the hook before the night's over. I can feel it."

"That's the name of the game, right?" I ask. "Are you ever too attached to a painting to sell it?"

"I start off too attached to all of them," she admits, her eyes darting from wall to wall like she's trying to count children running amok on the playground. "And then somewhere along the line there's a total disconnect. It's like I never painted it in the first place. Sometimes I can't remember where it all began or how it ended up on canvas."

"Does that disconnect coincide with being immersed in something new? You let go of a painting to make room for what's next?"

"Sometimes," Osla explains. "But usually, it just happens. And then I feel lighter, and I actually like the idea of someone else being moved by it."

"And paying for it!" Arden interrupts, smiling. "That must ease the sting of letting go."

"Sure," Osla says. "I've been lucky all this somehow manages to pay the bills. But I've also been known to give away a painting or two."

"Shh," Arden says. "I think there are still some interested prospects roaming around. We don't want to give 'em any ideas." Osla scans the room again, shaking her head at Arden.

"We're going out when this wraps up," Arden says to me. "Sort of an impromptu after-party. Want to join us?"

"Sounds like a plan," I say.

"Good," she says. "That's great. I wasn't sure if you had to go home early to get ready for tomorrow."

"No, all set. I'm always ready."

"Ready for what?" Osla asks, tuning back into our conversation.

"John's a tugboat captain," Arden explains. "He heads out for two weeks tomorrow."

"I love that idea," Osla says, her eyes brightening. "Imagine . . . two whole weeks at sea to work in peace."

"Something like that," I say, hoping Arden won't bring up my music. Luckily, the room is just starting to clear, so she switches back into flutter mode.

"We'll head out in less than thirty," she says, walking toward the door. I can see Chase waiting for her there, with Macy standing next to him, holding Garrett's hand. Arden talks to them for a moment before bending down to give Garrett a hug. Chase puts a hand on Arden's shoulder, nods his head at something she says, and then kisses her on the cheek. The kiss is so quick that it doesn't even look like his lips actually touched her face.

I'm relieved they're leaving and won't be at the party. At this point, I don't think it means much that Arden invited me to tag along, but I'd still rather not have Chase there.

As I walk to the restaurant with Osla, she grills me about tugboats. I know she isn't thinking about biting winds, monotonous days, or the rusty patches being a sailor leaves on the hull of your life. No, Osla's like everyone else who's drawn to the sense of rugged independence and raw beauty of life at sea, not to mention the image of a brightly colored tugboat tirelessly, even cheerfully, pulling something toward its destination.

Osla wants to know about the people I work with. She asks their names (Little Hal, Marakesh, Joe Joe James)and what they did before they worked on tugs (soap sculptor, snow removal specialist, and convicted felon). I'm having a hard time staying focused. It's all a bit of a blur to me anyway—information I don't even realize I hold onto after my feet hit the dock.

Once we duck inside, the glow of the restaurant helps me settle down. It's like we just walked into someone's living room—low tables, couches, and high-backed chairs with ottomans. I want to sit near Arden to avoid reaching new heights in small talk, but I'm not sure how to orchestrate that without offending Osla and her guests. Standing at the bar to get a drink seems like a solid strategy to buy me some time.

"What can I get for you, Osla?"

"Vodka, warm," she says, squeezing my arm before she sits down at the long table with a *Reserved* sign on it. I see a few people from the gallery walking in, and soon their collective murmur envelops Osla.

I keep glancing at the door while I wait for my drink order. Osla is already motioning for me to come over and join her fan club. I pick up our drinks and walk over as unhurriedly as I can without appearing to be moving in slow motion.

When I get to the middle of the room, the door whooshes open. The whole crowd turns, as I do, to see who's responsible for the cascade of laughter that follows. Arden. And Chase. They're laughing uncontrollably, almost holding each other up.

Osla practically skips over to Arden. "Do tell," she says, giving her a hug. "*What* is so funny?"

Arden and Chase exchange sideways glances. "Nothing we can even begin to explain," Arden says. "Don't mean to be evasive, but it's a long, sordid story."

"Sordid, yes," Chase agrees, coughing now from laughing so hard. "You can say that again."

"John!" Arden's smile fades as she takes me in. "Hi!"

I'm starting to get a *you're such a pal, John* feeling. It isn't a sensation I've experienced often, but it doesn't take long for me to remember how much it sucks. And what is Arden doing laughing like that anyway? Isn't she overwrought with grief?

I blurt out an effortless lie. "Glad I have a chance to say good-bye. I got a call and have to be at the dock earlier than expected, so I'll be heading home after this drink."

Osla looks devastated, a sure sign that she's already imagining what it would be like to slip into my life for a while.

Arden seems nonplussed. "Bummer," she says. "We didn't even get to talk tonight."

"I had a great time. Really. Thanks for inviting me." I take two long swigs of beer and walk over to leave my bottle on the bar. When I walk back to say good-bye, I see Chase on the pay phone by the door with his head down.

"What's going on?" I ask Arden.

"Chase brought Garrett and Aunt Macy home, and something seemed off," Arden explains, biting her bottom lip. "Garrett's mom was shaking, but she wouldn't say what was upsetting her. Chase left them the number to the restaurant in case they needed anything, and the bartender just passed him a message. I'm not sure what's happening."

"Is your family in some sort of trouble?"

Arden nods her head. "Garrett lives with my Aunt Macy and his mom, my cousin Marva. His dad is a heroin addict with a habit of harassing them."

"So Chase is going to . . ." I'm not sure I want to know how Chase fits into this picture.

"Chase takes dance lessons from Aunt Macy. One night she gave him a glimpse of what they've been dealing with on the Levi front, which is remarkable to me, because she and Marva don't open up to many people. To *any* people, really. Anyway, Chase is trying to help them sort through it all."

"He's quite a guy, that Chase.".

"Yeah, he is quite a guy." Arden looks over at him, an unreadable expression face. "Well, you've got to shove off, and I'm going to say a quick hello to Osla while Chase is still on the phone. Thanks for coming down."

I know Arden is distracted and overwhelmed, but it feels like her good-bye is as dismissive as it sounds. I wave to Chase on my way out and step onto the sidewalk, all stirred up with no place to go. I can't wait to get home so I can fall asleep, wake up, and be gone.

Chapter Nine: Arden

Tuesday, May 17 & Wednesday, May 18, 1994

I'm exhausted. For a few hours I'd been buoyant, riding the wave of an opening gone right. The gallery had been filled with an ideal mix of boldface names, media, and fresh faces, and a robust flurry of open checkbooks before the night wound down.

The first bit of air escaped from my balloon when Chase came back to the gallery walk me to the after-party. I was sideswiped by the memory of Billy's laughter, how tears would stream down his face, and he'd shake like unbridled joy was bouncing around inside him. Striding down the sidewalk with Chase was no place for my tears, so I'd blinked hard to savor the memory for one more moment before willing my eyes to stop glistening.

When we got to the restaurant and John announced his early exit, I thought I caught an unsettling, barely detectable hint of disappointment in his voice. I couldn't be sure and didn't have the headspace to dwell on it. I intended to plant myself next to Osla to circumvent a repeat performance of her last after-party, when she ordered rounds of vodka shots for anyone who was still vertical, but then the drama at Aunt Macy's took center stage.

I'm used to things being different at my aunt's place. While my mom thrives on order and routine trumps all, whimsy rules at Aunt Macy's. Her clocks may keep time, but they definitely don't control how she spends it. When I was a kid, she'd make breakfast in bed for dinner, roll up the carpet so I could practice the worm, and enthusiastically taste my tomato sauce and sardine popsicles or the blue cheese dressing and gummy worm soup I'd concoct while she watched soap operas and folded laundry.

Even after Marva was born, Aunt Macy didn't succumb to the routines and pressures of parenthood. I never saw her in a spit up–stained T-shirt. She always left her apartment wearing stacked heels and ruby red lips.

The one exception to her being pulled together was when her life with Uncle Chester was falling apart. My behind-the-couch reading fort was prime eavesdropping real estate, and I was eleven when I overhead Aunt Macy telling Mom how she came home to discover Marva's teenage babysitter on Uncle Chester's lap. There were no sobs or bursts of anger, but for a few weeks after Aunt Macy gave him the boot, she played the same album—Roberta Flack's *Blue Lights in the Basement*—over and over and only left the apartment to teach at the studio or take Marva out to get some fresh air.

I remember worrying and wondering how long someone could survive on Roberta Flack alone. Then one day, Aunt Macy and I were back to wearing Halloween costumes to the park in March and ordering our lunch at the corner deli in pig Latin.

It's no surprise that Marva was a free spirit from day one. Her given name was "Marvelous," after all, and Aunt Macy encouraged Marva to let curiosity be her guide. This resulted in a wonder-filled childhood, but it also catapulted Marva into Levi's orbit when she was only fifteen.

I remember Aunt Macy and Marva having a heated conversation while we were all huddled in their kitchen cleaning up after Thanksgiving dinner. "I'm more than a little worried about you and that man, baby girl. Have you stopped to think about why he wants to be friends with a fifteen-year-old? You know, the law doesn't tolerate grown men stepping out with girls your age."

"That *man* has a name," Marva had said, turning off the faucet to face her mother. "It's Levi C. James, and I won't let you try to make it sound like he has ulterior motives. Levi is the best thing that's ever happened to me. I'm an old soul. You said so yourself, Mom. We are *friends*. Got that? *Friends*." She'd assumed the classic, pissed-off teen stance, eyes ablaze and arms folded tightly across her chest.

Aunt Macy hadn't looked up to see the challenge in Marva's gaze. "I knew I should've stood up to your father when he insisted that we name you *Marva* after your grandfather's first love," she'd said, gently clinking piece after piece of silverware into a drawer.

"You mean Uncle Chester's mom?" I'd asked, wondering how I could change the subject before real sparks flew.

"No, his grandfather's first love and Chester's mom were two different people," Aunt Macy had explained. "So somehow Chester got it in his head that if we named our sweet baby girl Marva, she would remember to be true to herself and not second-guess her heart. What kind of logic is that, you ask?" She nodded at each of our blank stares. "*Exactly.*"

"You are insane, Mom. What the hell does my name have to do with anything?"

"I think . . . well, this isn't the time to get into all that," she'd replied. "You know how I get off track when I'm worked up. I just start spewing, and it's Thanksgiving, so . . ."

That's when Marva had walked over to hug Macy from behind. "I want you to stop spewing and stewing and whatever else you're doing. I am *happy*. Levi's an angel, and he says my name is Marva because I am *marvelous*."

I remember being glad that Marva couldn't see her mother's face. Aunt Macy looked like she was bracing herself for a sad scene in a movie she'd watched so many times that she knew it by heart.

I don't remember any *I told you sos* or heavy sighs the following year when Marva announced her pregnancy. Levi disappeared two days later, and Aunt Macy rolled up her sleeves. It didn't take long for Marva to realize that life with Levi wouldn't be a life she'd want to live. By then, his "side jobs" had escalated into a full-blown drug-dealing operation, with more sampling than Marva liked to admit. So by the time Levi left, Marva was more relieved than heartbroken.

Even after he moved to Idaho with another woman, Levi made it clear that he didn't want any other men in Marva's life. He called constantly to grill her about who she was spending time with, when in reality, Marva's life didn't leave room for anything other than two jobs and Garrett.

Tonight, when the bartender walks over and asks if any of us knows Chase Sommers, I hold my breath. Aunt Macy is the opposite of a drama queen; in fact, she hates asking for help. And the message she's left for Chase is sparse. *Please call.*

For a moment, I'm caught between Osla pulling me toward her posse and John acting slightly bruised as he slinks toward the door. Then it's as if a giant spotlight is closing in on Chase hunched over at the pay phone. The rest of the room mutes as I walk over to stand by him. He grabs my hand, interlacing his fingers with mine.

I glance over at Osla's table. Everyone is passing plates of food around the table, oblivious to the rest of the room. "Not good?" I whisper as Chase hangs up.

"Macy says Levi's on his way, and he's threatening to take Garrett with him." Chase runs his fingers through his hair and leaves his palm resting on top of his head. "What do you think? Is he full of shit?"

"Aunt Macy's instincts are spot on. Does she think Levi's for real?"

Chase nods. "She does. I need to get over there. It's hard to talk about this over the phone."

I wonder why Aunt Macy left the message for Chase instead of me? Was she worried about interrupting my important night, or did she just have more faith in Chase? It doesn't matter. Even though I've only known him for a few weeks, I can see that the way Chase makes everything seem all right is something a person could get used to. What it would be like to get lost in his steadiness? I can't imagine not spinning.

"Thank you," I say, giving his hand a squeeze, "for making this infinitely better than it would be if you weren't such a great friend." I stretch up to kiss his cheek and catch the very corner of his mouth. I also catch an odd expression crossing his face, but it's replaced with a genuine smile too quickly for me to be sure. My emotional compass has been working overtime all night, and I'm tired of wondering what direction everyone else is heading. Hell, I'm tired of trying to figure out where I'm heading.

"I'll just sneak out," Chase says.

"Sure, yes, go. I'll be right behind you. Let me say some good-byes and tell the restaurant manager to keep the drinks flowing on my tab."

"You don't have to rush out. I'll . . ."

"Chase," I interrupt. "Do you actually think it's OK that you drop everything to meet me for cocktails and sympathy and then jump in to help my family—within the same day, mind you—and then I just hang out at a party?"

"Are you always keeping score?" he asks, looking truly puzzled. "It doesn't work that way—or feel that way—to me. And hey, we're both tired and worried right now, so let's not start analyzing everything. I gotta go now. Stay here or don't. I'll talk to you later either way."

Before I can recover from the keeping-score comment, he's gone. How am I going to slide back into any semblance of conversation? A hot ball of anxiety is traveling up from my stomach into my throat, the same one I remember feeling when Casey told me how her dad would lock her mom in the pantry or make her sit motionless at the kitchen table for hours until he gave her permission to move.

"Arden!" Osla calls. "I've been keeping a seat warm for you. What's going on over there?"

"Chase had to go take care of something."

"And John?"

"John has an early morning."

"If you're inspired, no morning is too early," she mumbles, not trying to hide her disappointment. Even though I think I have my finger on the pulse of the evening, I still missed the obvious. Osla is interested in more than John's life at sea; she's hot for him.

"For a tugboat captain, that may not be the case," I counter. "When they're on, they've got to be on."

"Don't you just seem to have the inside scoop?" Osla raises an eyebrow.

"No inside scoop here."

"Does he have a girlfriend?"

"Still no scoop. But he hasn't mentioned anyone."

She raises her eyebrow again. "I'm surprised, Arden. You usually have the lowdown on everyone."

"John and I really just met this week. Even though we're from the same hometown, we didn't have an actual conversation until a few days ago."

"And he hasn't mentioned anyone?"

I shake my head. "It's been an intense time for both of us. A mutual friend died suddenly . . . accidentally."

"Oh, I didn't know, Arden," Osla whispers, rubbing the top of my arm. "Why didn't you tell . . . ? Well, enough prying. John is *very* intriguing to me, but I don't mean to sound like a stalker."

"You don't sound like a stalker. You sound *interested*. Let me do some digging for you."

Her eyes flash as she bounces back toward the table. "You're good, Arden. *Really* good."

Really good? Debatable. Really turned upside down? For sure. I feel buried under a landslide of questions. Is Chase at Aunt Macy's apartment yet? What's going on inside Garrett's head right now? Is Levi really on his way? Why did John's exit feel like a door closing?

That's when I hit the wall. Time to leave. I say my good-byes and seamlessly go from the restaurant into a cab to my apartment, where my plan is to run in and change into different clothes en route to Aunt Macy's. Instead, I find Chase sitting on the front steps of my building.

"What's going on?" I ask, plopping down next to him. "Your expression has me worried."

"It's going from bad to worse over there. They're petrified."

"They think Levi's really coming back?"

"He says he's on his way, and no one can keep him away from his son. He last called from Chicago, so theoretically he could be in New York by tomorrow afternoon. He's still threatening to take Garrett back to Idaho with him. "

"It doesn't help that he's delivered on his threats before," I say. I can tell by his expression that Chase is in the dark on the details of Levi's last visit. "A few months ago, Levi was in town and told Marva he'd cut all her hair off if she didn't take him back. Then he barged into their apartment, pushed Marva up against a wall and hacked off her ponytail in front of Aunt Macy. They didn't know Garrett witnessed the whole scene until Levi was gone."

"I didn't realize . . . we've got to get them out of there," Chase says. "And we've got to call the police. If he cut her hair off last time, who knows what he's capable of?"

"They don't want to go into hiding, and good luck convincing them to call the police."

"I know they can't hide forever, but they can hide until the situation is diffused. It's better than being sitting ducks, especially if they won't call the cops. Have they ever?"

"Marva did. Once, but she didn't want to. She's afraid it's just going to make Levi angrier."

"What did the police do?"

"They didn't have a chance to do anything. When they put her on hold to transfer the call, she hung up."

"She hung up? That's it? I'm sorry, Arden, but the police *have* to be involved. And Marva, Macy, and Garrett need to get the hell out of their apartment."

"They've thought about places to go before. I mean, my parents' door is always open, but we all know it's also probably the first place Levi would look." I feel a twinge of nervousness. "And my mom's in the dark about all this. So there's that."

I'm glad Chase doesn't want to know why my mom has no idea what's going on. "Any family or friends Levi doesn't know about?" he asks.

"Or maybe I could rent them a hotel room somewhere?" He pauses. "With an asshole like Levi, something offshore would be ideal, huh?"

"Yeah, right," I agree. "Offshore."

Some light bulbs take longer than others to turn on. When mine finally starts to glow, I do too. "That . . . is . . . it. Exactly. Garrett can go out on the tugboat with John."

Silence.

"John leaves for two weeks tomorrow. Whether or not Levi's bluffing, we'll have time to help them deal with the situation."

"Two weeks on a tugboat?" Chase asks. "John doesn't even know Garrett."

"What are you talking about? They met each other tonight. Garrett seemed smitten."

"That's right, *Garrett* was smitten, but I think that was probably more with the idea of a tugboat. And John, he's a single guy who probably doesn't have much experience with kids. Oh yeah, and maybe—just maybe—a tugboat isn't the safest place in the world for an eight-year-old boy."

"It sounds a hell of a lot safer than staying where he is," I counter defensively as I fish around my bag for my keys, "and I think John would be great with Garrett."

Chase stands to follow me through the front door and into the elevator. Murray, the super, pokes his head out from his office. "'Night, Arden."

" 'Night, Murray."

"Let's think this through," Chase says as we shoot up to the sixth floor. "Garret's mom doesn't know John. When is that introduction supposed to take place? As the tug pulls away from the dock?"

"Will you at least consider taking my idea seriously?" This is starting to feel like an actual argument. Our first. "Don't discount it until you hear me out."

"OK, Arden," he says, running both hands through his hair. "Let me have it."

"Here it is, step by step," I say, ready to improvise. "Step one, I call John to see if he'll let Garrett stow away on the tug. If he agrees, we'll talk to Aunt Macy and Marva, see if they'll let Garrett go."

"That would be step two," Chase says, holding up two fingers.

"Glad you're still with me. Step three, we talk to Garrett. A short conversation, he'll want to start packing. Step four, John and Garrett head out, and we have some time to figure this out."

"We?" Without looking, I can feel him staring at me.

"Yes, we. You, me, Marva, Aunt Macy . . . we." I unlock my door and lead the way inside. "I know you've started to really care about Garrett and Aunt Macy." Chase looks deflated, and I realize he expected my response to be more grounded in the two of us. "You're too quiet right now. What are you thinking?"

"I'm thinking that this is the only idea we have on the table right now," he says. "Unless you're sure we shouldn't be pushing them to stay in a hotel or get them to reconsider camping out at your parents' place."

I take a deep breath. "A hotel room, I guess that could be a last resort, but I don't know. And my mom, well Aunt Macy doesn't want her to know what's going on with Levi."

"You mean your mom doesn't know what he did to Marva's hair?"

"Mom thought Marva got a pixie haircut by choice, and Aunt Macy is determined to protect her sister because . . ." How many times have I searched for the right word, any words to describe how Mom would break? ". . . she's fragile."

"Fragile as in . . ."

"Fragile as in she had a nervous breakdown," I say, knowing the words were going to keep tumbling out now whether I wanted them to or not. "Make that nervous breakdowns. She's been hospitalized a few times, and Aunt Macy still creeps around on eggshells, afraid Mom won't be able to deal with bad news."

"I'm so sorry, Arden. I had no idea."

"There's nothing for you to be sorry about. Mom seems hardier these days. Even when Billy died, she didn't disappear into her room for days."

Billy. I can remember his *Go to the police; go directly to the police* reaction when I told him about Levi. To Billy, doing anything other than that was reckless, and even though I agreed with him, Marva and Aunt Macy stayed unwavering in their belief that getting the cops involved would only make Levi's rage escalate.

As Chase and I talk, time seems to become thicker, heavier, more tangible. "I'm going to give John a call. Garrett may not even be allowed on the boat, so before we start worrying about anything else, let's start with that."

"Let's start by seeing if John is up to the task," Chase says.

"I wouldn't use the word *task*, Chase."

"An eight-year-old boy on a tugboat for two weeks?" Chase stands, reaching both of his arms toward the ceiling. "Yeah, that's what you call a task. But you're right. Let's start with a phone call."

I feel Chase's hand on my shoulder as I pick up the receiver. "I'm sorry for getting snappy," he says. "I'm not used to hearing brilliant ideas in the middle of the night." I appreciate that he's trying to smooth things over.

"Brilliant, I like that." I pause with my hand on the receiver. "I just realized I don't know John's number."

"You don't know his number?" Chase sounds a little relieved.

"I have it, but it's written down at my office. My assistant found it for me this morning."

"You're willing to send your young cousin out to sea with a guy you don't even know well enough to have his phone number? *So* not a crazy idea."

"Oh, stop it, would you? I don't have to know his phone number to know what kind of person he is. John is a solid guy. He's kind. He's responsible. He's . . ."

"OK, OK," Chase says, taking his hand off my shoulder. "You sound like the president of his fan club."

"If I was the president of his fan club, I'd know his number, wouldn't I?" I smirk. "So, I'll dial information. That's what it's for, right?"

"What's his last name? Do you even know that?"

"Yes, wise guy. Raymond. His name is John Raymond."

"I'm sure there's only one John Raymond in Manhattan."

"I know where he lives—approximately. That's something." I dial information. "Raymond, John Raymond. It would be a Chelsea or Meatpacking District address."

I wait while the operator searches. There are two John Raymonds, a J-o-h-n and a J-o-n. There are also four J. Raymonds. As A. *McHale*, I know those are probably women, so I decided to call J-o-h-n Raymond first. The phone rings five times. I almost hang up when a gravelly voice answers, "Hello?"

"Jackpot!" I say. "John, hi, it's me, Arden."

"Arden? What are you doing calling . . ."

I finish his sentence, "at two in the morning? I know. It's late. Or early. But I really need to talk to you. And even though I left your number at the office, I got lucky with 411. Geez, it seems like every time I call you, I start to ramble. Let me take a deep breath." In. Out. I can feel Chase watching me. "OK," I continue, "Now I need *you* to take a deep breath and hear me out, John." As I make my pitch, I have to admit that the idea sounds way more outlandish than it did inside my head."

"You just came up with that?" John asks. "Since I left you a few hours ago?"

"More like in the last thirty minutes. The situation at Aunt Macy's escalated, and there aren't a lot of options. Chase said something about offshore and then *bam*, you popped into my head." I look over at Chase, who's still sitting on my couch, pretending to be interested in the books stacked every which way on the shelves next to him.

"Shit," John says. "This sounds like something out of a movie."

"It feels like a bad movie right now, but I know we'll be able to figure things out. Levi's latest threat is like a catalyst, making everyone realize we can't go on pretending everything's OK when it won't be until we stop letting him terrorize them."

"I understand," John says. "I, uh . . . I need to think about everything you just said."

"Do you want me to call you back? In a few minutes?"

John laughs. "Have you ever considered a career in sales?"

"PR is sales, and if I've learned anything, it's that persistence pays off."

"I want to help," John says. "I really do." He lets out a quick sigh. "OK. Here's the deal. I'll need to meet his mom and to talk directly with Garrett to make sure he's up for this. You all need to understand that I won't be able to just bring him back, especially if I'm offshore."

"Wait, so will Garrett be your guest or more like a stowaway? I mean . . . can you get in trouble for this?"

"Trouble? Only if you call losing my job trouble."

"I can't ask you to put your job in jeopardy, John. We'll figure something else out."

"You didn't ask me to put my job in jeopardy. And you know Billy wouldn't think twice about this. He'd put the kid in his damn sea bag and sneak him aboard if he had to. I'm in, Arden. We'll make it work."

"You won't have to worry about Garrett. He's a pretty resilient kid, and he's used to going with the flow."

"Yeah, well, going with the flow and being *in* the flow are two very different things," John says. "It's lonely out there. And my crew is . . ." he pauses to find the right word, "eclectic. There's bad weather, bad food, and long stretches of going nowhere slowly. And when I'm on watch, I won't be able to entertain him."

"He's used to entertaining himself," I say. "I know he loves to play with LEGOs."

"LEGOs on a tugboat. *That* sounds like a good time all around." John laughs.

"What time does the boat leave the dock tomorrow?" I ask.

"Sometime around four."

"In less than two hours? You weren't exaggerating about having an early start."

"Four *p.m.*," he says.

"I thought you said you had to leave the party because you were taking off early."

"That memory of yours is something else," John teases.

I ignore him. "Four is great. That gives us plenty of time to make this happen."

"Oh, yeah, plenty."

"How about we meet at my Aunt Macy's apartment at seven thirty?"

"Works for me."

I give John the address. "See you in the morning."

"It's already morning, Arden."

"See you later then," I say. "And thank you."

I hang up and collapse on the couch, believing that maybe my idea isn't so crazy after all. I hand the phone to Chase so he can call Aunt Macy, knowing that the idea will have a better chance of survival if it comes from him.

Chapter Ten: John

Wednesday, May 18, 1994

Arden's voice takes me from zero to sixty in a matter of seconds. I'm dozing on the couch when the phone rings, and my first thought is that my departure plans might be changing. When I hear Arden instead of a dispatcher, my just-awake brain shifts into speculation mode. Is she calling because she wishes I didn't leave the party so early?

I soon learn *no* is the answer to that question and any others swirling around my still-groggy head. Arden is calling on me to be a lifesaver. She dives right into the scenario, and even though it's difficult to follow at first, I don't have to hear much to understand how very much this means to her.

She mentions Chase, so I know he must be nearby, maybe even holding her hand or holding *her* while she's talking to me. I have to block out that image to focus on what she's proposing. I may not be a *yes* person, but I can't turn my back on a kid in trouble. And even though I keep trying to sidestep it, there's something magnetic about Arden.

Can Garrett come out on the tug with me? Sure. Can I handle being responsible for him for two weeks? Yes. Could I lose my job over this? Absolutely, but also unlikely. Did I want to do it? *Yes* is the word that surfaces. I don't have to summon it up; I just have to let it out.

As Arden explains her idea, I sense the scheme doesn't feel as solid to her spoken aloud. I wonder why she doesn't send Garrett out to her parents' house in Greenport or take him to Disney World. But more than anything, I feel grateful that she thought of me. I've gone from someone on the periphery of her life to a person she's leaning on to solve a problem. She trusts me.

I put my head back on the pillow and listen to Arden breathe as she waits for my decision. Her call answers the questions that have been banging around in my head since I left the gallery.. *Do I want to see Arden again? Do I want to try to let her in?* Yes.

* * *

I never drift back to sleep, and I get out of bed before six to make coffee. As I get dressed and listen for it to bubble up into the metal pot, I know the real moment of truth will be when I need to be alert in the wheelhouse from midnight to 6 a.m.

My conversation with Arden still seems dreamlike. Part of me wants to call her so she knows I was coherent when I agreed to meet them at Macy's apartment. That's when I realize that I don't know her number. She's going to show up at Garrett's at seven thirty and expects me to be there too, even if I do have a change of heart.

I'm relieved that calling isn't an option. What if it was, and I could hear Chase's voice in the background when she answered? I don't want to know if they spent the night together. Chase seems like a decent guy, and I can't blame him for trying to make it clear that he considers Arden to be off limits. I'm sure he suspects that I'm attracted to her. Who wouldn't be? Chase may not even consider me a threat, believing it would take a different kind of guy to pique her interest.

Enough, I think as I tuck a handheld VHF radio under my arm and head downstairs to hail a cab. The radio is a last-minute idea, and I think it might actually be a deal maker. If Garrett's family knows they'll have a way to communicate with him beyond an occasional pay phone call, they'll feel more at ease.

My cab whizzes through increasingly crowded streets. The city is in acceleration mode, and I'm feeling ahead of the curve. When the driver pulls over at the address Arden gave me, I spot Chase already standing outside the building. Alone.

"Good morning," he says, opening the door and extending his hand as I step out. Chase has a great handshake—strong, genuine, and filled with the confidence of having never doubted himself.

"Good morning."

"This is really great of you, John. When Arden came up with the idea, I was skeptical, but then after you bought into it, I started to think it just might work."

"I don't need anyone to thank me. If I can help keep a little boy safe and give his family and friends some peace of mind, I'm happy to do whatever I can."

"Arden should be here any minute," he says. "I called her before I left to tell her I was en route." *Yes.*

"Anything I need to know before we head in? Have they called the police already?"

"I've learned that the police are not a popular subject in this household."

"But if they really think Levi is on his way to kidnap Garrett, then we should . . ."

"I don't know whether or not we can believe Levi, but he does call every few hours. Last time he said he was barreling across Illinois," Chase says. "At least he's either afraid to fly or completely incapable of making a plane reservation, so even though he's harassing them over the phone, he can't appear out of thin air."

"We need to convince Marva and Macy to call the police."

"I'm with you on that," he says, running both hands through his thick mop of sandy blonde hair. I hear someone shout, "Hey, guys!" and turn to see Arden running down the sidewalk. She gives each of us a hug before grabbing both of my hands. "*You* are a rock star, Captain Raymond. Let's get in there and make this happen."

When Arden presses 4B, the front door immediately buzzes open. Seems a bit loose on the security end to me. What if we were Levi instead of the Three Musketeers?

The hallway is dark and musty. I take a deep breath as we wind our way up the staircase. "What's with the radio?" Arden asks.

"It's to show Garrett's family they'll be able to stay in touch while he's on the tug. Not always, but when we're nearby, which could be a lot of the time."

Arden lightly punches my shoulder. "Genius!" she says, grinning broadly. "That is *genius*." Her eyes widen as she says, "I just realized something. Garrett is going to experience the Wheelhouse Café live and in person."

"What's the Wheelhouse Café?" Chase asks.

I shoot Arden a hard-edged look. I thought she'd been joking about not being able to keep a secret. "Oh, shit," she says. "I'm an idiot."

"You warned me." I try to sound nonchalant. "The Wheelhouse Café is a floating performance venue," I begin, not having to elaborate since we're standing outside the apartment.

As Chase goes to knock, the door swings open. "Good morning, Macy," he says.

Macy looks at me with a blank expression that makes it impossible for me to decipher what's going on beneath her surface. "Good to see you again," I say, extending my hand, which she takes and shakes while keeping her eyes locked with mine.

I'd forgotten to ask Arden how much they already knew—had she shared the plan with them, or just that we had one?

"Grandma! Are they here *already*?" a voice screeches from inside the apartment.

"It *is* seven thirty," Macy says without raising her voice. "Who knew punctuality still existed?" She winks at Chase and motions for us to come in. We shuffle single file onto the faded violet Oriental rug and stand in an awkward row.

The apartment looks just-pulled together—every pillow in place, and mugs lined up on a shiny blue tray on the coffee table. I smell the large rosemary plant in the corner before I see it, and breathe it in deeply. Rosemary is supposed to be exhilarating, but something about its scent puts me at ease.

"What is this, a lineup?" Macy asks. "Sit down, sit down. Make yourselves comfortable. Marva and Garrett will be right out. Or at least Garrett will."

As we squeeze in next to each other on the couch, I hear the soft hum of music coming from one of the rooms. I assume it's Marva's, and then she emerges from it wearing pink floral scrubs. "Hi, Arden. I understand you have a bright idea and the only thing I could use more than that right now is a good night's sleep." She stops in front of me. "You must be John. Hi. I'm anxious to hear what the three of you have cooked up."

That answers my question. We're going to lay it all out right now, and I wonder which one of us will be at the helm.

"You're right, I'm John. And I'm glad to be able to help. Garrett's a great kid."

As if on cue, Garrett comes bounding out of his room. He hugs Arden first and then climbs up Chase's back for a piggyback ride. Arden stands on her tiptoes to look him in the eye. "We're here to talk to your mom and Grandma Macy while you eat breakfast."

"What are you doing here?" Garrett asks, looking up at me.

"I'm Captain John. We met . . ."

"I *know* who you *are*," Garrett says. "You're the tug guy. How could I forget you?"

Garrett scoots into the kitchen. I can hear him dragging a chair across the floor, and then I catch a glimpse of him standing on it as he reaches up to grab cereal out of a cabinet.

"So, sit," Marva says. "Please. Sit down and fill us in."

"Has Levi called again?" Chase asks.

"About thirty minutes ago. He said he was in Ohio. And he was nastier than ever." Marva is pacing.

"First, I want you to relax and know that everyone is going to be safe—Garrett, you, and Macy." As Chase continues, Marva nods slowly. "Then, I want you to listen to this idea and know that I'm behind it 100 percent."

"OK," Marva says, sitting down on the end table next to Chase.

Chase talks to Marva as if they're alone in the room. He tells her the plan and shows her the radio. She glances over at me a couple of times, not sizing me up exactly, but her *I wonder* wheels are definitely spinning.

When Chase finishes, Arden opens her mouth as if she's going to say something, and then she closes it again. "What is it, Arden?" Marva asks.

"I was going to say that John's from my hometown. That he comes from a nice family, and he's a responsible, kind person who didn't hesitate when I asked if he'd do this."

"I don't know," Marva says. "It's hard to imagine."

"Hard to imagine Garrett on the tugboat?" Arden asks.

"Yes," she says, "and even harder to imagine how angry Levi will be if he barges in and Garrett's not here."

"Listen, Marva," Chase says, "you and Macy won't be here to find out. You're going to lay low, stay with someone, somewhere he won't be able to track you down."

"He doesn't know where I work. I have a new job," Marva says, sounding hopeful. "At least, I don't think he's figured it out."

I can hear Garrett whistling as he rinses out his cereal bowl. He hasn't been lurking on the fringes of the room, trying to decipher what all the commotion is about. I take it as a good sign that our early-morning entourage disrupting his usual routine hasn't made him anxious. I can tell that this kid trusts the people who love him to take care of him. He's going to be all right.

Chapter Eleven: Arden

Wednesday, May 18, 1994

I relax the moment Chase starts sharing the plan with Marva and Aunt Macy. Their expressions stay calm and open, and they don't interrupt him, which in itself is nothing short of a miracle. They just might believe that Garrett would be in good hands with John.

In fact, he would be in hands I can't stop staring at. John clasped them together when Chase started talking, and now he's leaning over to rest his elbows on his knees. John's fingers are long, and his skin is a toasty color that radiates warmth. I start to imagine what it would feel like to have those hands cradling my face or unbuttoning my shirt. *Enough.* What am I *doing* besides completely losing track of what Chase is saying?

"Marva," I say too loudly, trying to startle myself into breaking the hand spell. "We need to move quickly. John leaves this afternoon around four, so if you're on board, we should talk to Garrett and then get him packed so he's ready to go."

"I understand," she says. "I think we should run this by Garrett now. Mom, what do you think?" Aunt Macy nods her head in agreement. I like how she is clearly letting Marva take the lead in making this decision.

"What will you tell the school?" I ask, thinking of this for the first time.

"I'll tell them we've had a family emergency, so Garrett will be out of town for a couple of weeks," Marva says. "That sounds good, right? And it's the truth." We all nod in unison.

Garrett raps his knuckles on the doorjamb. "Knock, knock. Can I come back in?"

"Get on over here, mister," Marva calls, opening her arms to him. "I want to tell you about a surprise in the works."

"For *me?*" Garrett squeals as she tickles him.

"For *you*," she says, swinging him around to face her. "Chase, Arden, Grandma Macy, and I all know how much you love tugboats."

"You got me a tugboat?" he screams, clapping his hands together. "No way! I don't *belieeeeeve* it!"

"You do dream big, don't you?" Aunt Macy says, chuckling.

"No tugboat?" Garrett directs this question at his mom with an exaggerated pout.

"Well, not in the way you're thinking, but in a way you've never imagined," Marva says. "*You* have been invited to go on a tugboat adventure with Captain Raymond."

Garrett looks at John, then back at his mother, then back at John. "For real? For *really* real?" He jumps up and starts doing a dance. Chase and John laugh aloud.

"For *really* real," John says. "I'd like you to come aboard as my chief mate."

"*Yes!*" he shouts, pumping his fist in the air. "This is gonna be *awesome*. I need to call Teddy and . . ."

"Wait a minute, young man," Marva says, pulling him back toward her. "This is a top secret mission."

"Super top secret," John says. "Only the people in this room will know where you are and what you're doing. Deal?" He sticks out one of his remarkable hands to grab Garrett's just when I think I've successfully dealt with that distraction.

"Deal," Garrett says, shaking John's hand wildly before holding his palm up. "High five too!"

John gives him a high five and then Marva, Chase, Garrett, and John start talking about what Garrett will need for the trip. Macy walks over to me and says, "I could use some help in the kitchen. Not that this wired group appears in need of caffeine."

I follow Aunt Macy, watch her fill the kettle and place it on the stove. She takes a bag of coffee out of the freezer and dumps some into the bottom of a glass pot. "So—you've got yourself in quite a quandary, don't you?" She doesn't direct this question at me, but even though I have no idea what she's alluding to, I do know I'm the only other person in the room."

"Quandary? What do you mean?"

"Two men on your mind," she says. "Two very *different* men who would both move mountains for you."

"I don't know what you're talking about," I say, annoyed that her comment is making me blush. "I'm not involved with either one of them . . . really."

"You don't have to say a word. I can sense it. You're on the brink of something, but you don't know what. Or even with who, for that matter!" Aunt Macy cracks herself up with that remark.

"I don't have time to think about this right now. I just lost one of my best friends, and I'm really concerned about Garrett. About all of you."

"You can't choose when love comes along," she says. "You just have to know how to listen to what your heart is trying to tell you. And that can be pretty tough if you're not used to the sound of your own voice."

"I *do* know the sound of my own voice," I say, all too aware that what I sound like a bratty toddler. "And, I know my own mind. You don't have to worry about me. You've got enough to focus on." I think about when Billy handed me that small blue box on my birthday. My mind had definitely been buckled into the driver's seat that day.

"We'll deal with Levi. I never doubted that. And it's not your *mind* I'm talking about, young lady. It's your *heart* that's the engine here, and I've got a feeling you haven't really paid attention to it before."

"I've been in love." My voice sounds softer and more unsure than I want it to.

"You *think* you've been in love is more like it. If you truly have been, chances are you'd still be." Aunt Macy stops suddenly and looks at me, stricken. "He's not *dead*, is he? You weren't in love with Billy, were . . ."

"No, no, the person I loved isn't dead. Or should I say *they're* not dead. We've all just moved on."

"Oh, now you've been in love with *multiple* people. Lucky girl," she chides, her hand poised to swipe the kettle off the burner just as it starts to whistle. "You can't just *move on* from love. This I know. When I met Chester, I was only seventeen. Do you think I wanted to be tied down to one man? I did not. I was seventeen! And I was something else back then. Beautiful. Brainy. Bold. But I just couldn't seem to leave his side. Marva came along when I was only nineteen, and then, well . . ."

"When did things change?" I ask.

"Things changed when Chester thought it was a good idea to have our babysitter sit on his lap," she says, with an exhale that makes her lower lip poke out. "Anyway, my point is that what I felt *wasn't* true love. It was infatuation with his face and his slow-talking sweetness and an idea of something I wasn't able to put my finger on but wanted to name so it would seem real." She pauses. "And I guess it was also youth making me feel like I had all this time."

"So have *you* ever been in love?"

"Not that I know of. But I don't plan on giving up anytime soon. I'm a woman who *loves* to look for love." She dances a little cha-cha, pulling me over to join her.

"I'm a woman who *loves* having an insane woman for an aunt," I say, moving my feet without much enthusiasm.

"You know, love can float right on by if you're not paying attention. Keep your heart open." She pours the water over the coffee. I can smell the dense aroma rising.

"Right now, I'm busy paying attention to that heavenly smell," I say.

"Well," Aunt Macy continues, "you've got not one but *two* fine men waiting in the wings . . . for you. I just might have to find it my heart to comfort the one you leave behind." Even when she's moving around the kitchen doing unsexy things, Aunt Macy looks like she's dancing—smooth, graceful, purposeful. She sways her hips and raises her eyebrows in a very un-aunt-like fashion.

That's when Chase calls out, "Arden! Could you come in here?"

I give Aunt Macy's arm a squeeze as I pass by. "Thanks for taking the time to talk to me about all this. You know Mom's not the most observant person and . . ." She puts her finger to my lips and winks.

"You rang?" I ask, sitting down between John and Chase.

"We think you should have the radio at your place since you're   right on the river. Marva and Macy can come over and talk to Garrett, but you'll be more comfortable with the technical side of things," Chase explains.

"I'll get the radio set up for you this morning and teach you how to use it," John continues.

Garrett starts hopping, hand raised, like he's trying to get his teacher's attention in class. "Captain John! Will I be able to *drive* the tugboat?"

"You will most definitely be at the helm from time to time," John says. "That's part of your duties as chief mate."

Garrett gallops around the room in a wide circle, chanting, "Yes, yes, yes, yes! This is going to be greater than great . . . the *greatest!*" I get dizzy watching him whirl about, but Garret's mad galloping doesn't seem to affect John. "We should get the radio set while you all get Garrett packed up," he says. "Chase, you want to come with us?"

"I do, yes," he says, "but I have to check in at the office for a couple of hours. Where should I meet you later?"

"Crew change is at Erie Basin at four," John says. "Could you bring Garrett down at three thirty with whoever else wants to be there to see him off? Erie Basin's in Red Hook at the very end of Columbia Street. You can't miss it. It's right near a big, old salvage barge."

"Got it," Chase says. "Marva, you heading to work?"

"Yeah, I should already be there, but I told them I'd be a little late this morning."

"OK," Chase says. "Macy, you help Garrett pack. I'll be back between two thirty and three to bring you both to the boat."

"We're on it," Aunt Macy says, ruffling Garrett's hair. "C'mon, sailor. Time for us to get a move on."

Everyone scatters, leaving John and I standing in the center of the living room. "Ready?" he asks.

"As I'll ever be," I say, scooping up my bag. Chase is waiting outside the door, and we follow him down the narrow staircase.

"Good job, Arden," Chase says, raising his arm so I can slap his palm.

"It was all you," I say. "I think my family would hang Garrett out a fourth-story window by his ankles if you told them it was the right thing to do."

"They may trust me, but it's clear those ladies are used to making up their own minds."

"Let's just keep moving forward," I say, meaning with the plan but also starting to feel dizzy on the descent. "There's a lot to do between now and this afternoon."

When we get to the ground floor, I realize John hadn't said a word on the way down. "You're quiet." I nudge him with my elbow. "Second thoughts?"

"Second thoughts? No," John answers with a crooked smile. "I'm just reminiscing about how soundly I was sleeping before you called me in the middle of the night."

"Ha," I say. "Let's go hail a cab, Mr. Funny."

"I'm going to take the subway to the office," Chase says. "We'll check in." He makes the subway announcement to both of us but most definitely directs *we'll check in* to me.

For the first time, I catch a glimpse of what Aunt Macy was talking about. Whether or not I want to be, I'm in between. For now, I'm relieved the choice of what to do next is clear: I'm heading home with John to learn about VHF marine band radios. It's as simple as that.

Chapter Twelve: John

Wednesday, May 18, 1994

For the first leg of our cab ride, silence reigns. Then we laugh as we simultaneously roll down our windows. "Stuffy in here, right?" Arden asks, her hair blowing up all around her as she pulls sunglasses out of her bag. She looks like a celebrity, not someone who would be in a battered old cab with a marine radio and me.

"*You* look like a movie star," I say.

"Really? Want my autograph?" She tilts her head back to strike a pose. "I'm the one who'll want *your* autograph when the next fourteen days are over. You're the one doing all the heavy lifting."

"Not too heavy. I'll be all right. Garrett's a good kid."

"Good, yes, but also eight. I consider myself to be a girl with boundless energy, but he's been known to make me feel like a sloth."

"The boat should calm him down a bit," I say, trying to remember the last time I spent time alone with a kid, and then realizing that would be never. "There's a rhythm to it. To life out there."

"I'm buying him a stack of books this afternoon," Arden says. "And some art supplies. A bon voyage present."

"Sounds like that's more of a present for me."

"What do you usually do when you're not performing?" she asks.

"I think you have the wrong idea about the Wheelhouse Café, and I don't want to mislead a potential fan. I don't play often. In fact, it's more like the opposite of often."

"You haven't misled me. I'm just fixated on this image of you hunkered down in the wheelhouse, mug of hot coffee at your side, guitar across your lap, and the salty night wrapped around you."

"Sometimes that's exactly right. Other times, I'll read. I eat. I exercise. I talk to the crew. I make lists."

"Of things to do?" she interrupts.

"Things to do or places I want to go, books I want to read."

"Do you work around the clock?"

"I stand two six-hour watches each day. Usually, the captain is on from 6 a.m. to noon and then 6 p.m. to midnight, but I like the midnight to six and noon to six. Suits me better."

"Seems like midnight to dawn would be the loneliest time."

"Depends on how you define lonely. For me, not so much."

Then Arden blurts out, "Do you have a girlfriend?" I can tell she's startled herself with her own question, because she quickly pretends to look out the window before adding, "Osla wants to know. She was grilling me for the scoop on all things Captain John Raymond after you bolted last night."

"Is that so?" I ask, amused at how wound up she's getting.

"Yeah, and she thought I was withholding information for my own devious purposes."

"You mean, to keep me all to yourself?" I ask, leaning toward her. I've always believed that the best time to push the envelope is when it's on the table right in front of you.

"Exactly," she says, relaxing a bit. "She gave me the third degree and was especially interested in finding out if you were attached to anyone. The poor woman was devastated that you left the party early."

"Good thing I left when I did so at least I got *some* sleep before my phone rang at 2 a.m."

"Think about what you just said and then think about how much sleep *I* got last night."

"Good point. I'm guessing not much, since you *stayed* at the party before concocting the scheme of the century."

"I haven't been sleeping lately, anyway. My mind won't stop racing with thoughts of Billy," she says, biting her bottom lip. "I wonder how long it's going to take for me to believe he's really gone."

I start to reach for her hand but press my palms into my thighs instead. "I don't have an answer for you, and I'm not going to repeat what people always say about how time heals, because it's not something I want to hear right now either."

"At least your friendship with Billy was intact. You have that." She looks up at me and sighs. "I know, I know. Stop beating myself up."

The cab slows to a stop in front of Arden's building. "Nice," I say. "Been here long?"

"Long enough," she answers, swinging the cab door open as a chubby, gray-haired man rushes out to get there first. "I beat you, Murray," Arden laughs. "How are you today?"

He tips his hat. "Infinitely better now that you're here, Miss McHale."

"You always make my day," she says, breezing into the building. "This is my friend, Captain John Raymond."

Murray stands at attention, saluting me. "Captain Raymond, a pleasure to meet you."

"You, too, Murray," I say. "And no salute necessary. I'm a tugboat captain."

"Even better!" Murray says. "Maybe you could take me out for a ride someday. It's something I've always wanted to do."

As the elevator doors slide together, Arden asks, "Does tugboat fascination know no limits?"

"What can I say? They're irresistible. Why do you think I ended up being a tugboat captain for so many years?"

"If people find out you can sing too, it will send them over the edge."

When I step into her apartment, I have to suppress my sudden urge to stretch out on her couch. Sure, having Arden lie down with me would be nice too, but just being in this room is enough for now. It's so quiet. My place can be as cleaned up as I can get it, and there will still be an undercurrent of chaotic energy, so I always take awhile to settle in.

"This I like," I say. "It feels like something out of a magazine. Like some sort of sanctuary."

"Thank you," Arden says. "That's a real compliment."

"Don't tell me a beautiful woman like you is used to getting fake ones?" Arden gives me as impish shrug as she shuffles through a stack of mail. "Let's think of a place to put this radio," I say. "My friend Charlie will come by later to put an antenna on the roof. That won't be a problem, will it?'

"You just met Murray. Nothing's a problem when it comes to making everyone around here happy."

"Roger that," I say. "How about on the desk by the window?"

"Excellent idea," she says, walking toward it.

I plug the radio in and watch all the lights turn on. "I'm sure you can figure out how to use the mic."

"Technical wizard that I am," she says, grabbing it from my hand. It feels good to have her right next to me. I wonder if she's making a conscious decision to stay still because she likes being close to me too, and then decide to pretend that's true when she leans in to me. "So, will I really be able to hear you sing?"

"Is that why you agreed to have the radio at your place?" I ask. "I *thought* you might have an ulterior motive."

"And what if I did?"

"I'm not one to disappoint my fans. I'll do my best to make sure you get to hear at least one Wheelhouse Café."

"Thank you," she says, taking a step back. I feel a cool pocket of air around me where she'd been. Is whispering *Come back* too desperate? I decide it is and say, "I never answered your question in the cab. I don't have a girlfriend."

"I'll be sure to give Osla the scoop. How about coffee and something to eat while you teach me about the radio?" she asks, heading into the kitchen.

"Whatever you've got in mind works for me," I say, wincing at how lame that sounds.

"Make yourself at home," she calls.

I hear her talking on the phone over the muffled backbeat of clinking glasses and other kitchen sounds. I take in the fireplace (working), then look at the paintings and photographs she has on the walls and leaning against stacks of books. No plants. I like that. My own black thumb makes it difficult for me to completely trust people with a knack for keeping plants alive, let alone helping them flourish.

I spot an acoustic guitar on a stand in the corner and am surprised Arden never mentioned that she plays. I consider going into the kitchen to ask her about it, but decide to take the guitar over to a chair by the window instead. I strum a song that reminds me of the peaceful feeling I'd only caught glimpses of before—the relief of being around someone who makes me feel like I'm exactly where I need to be.

Chapter Thirteen: Arden

Wednesday, May 18, 1994

I watch my answering machine light blink with imagined intensity, knowing only Mom would call so early. I decide to sneak in a return call while I figure out what to make for John. I don't think either of us is hungry, but I needed to retreat to a quiet space to stop reeling inside.

I catch my mom on her way out the door, so she's even more distracted than usual. I hope that means I'll get the highlights without the extended play-by-play, but Mom is in detail heaven. Right in the middle of a story about the eggplants she picked this morning, I hear John quietly strumming the guitar I hadn't played since junior high but couldn't bear to get rid of. He's singing a song about a pretty lady from Baton Rouge.

I hurry Mom off the phone and lean against the counter to listen. As much as I want to peek around the corner to watch John sing, I don't want to risk interrupting him.

That's when the shrill kettle stops John midverse. "Damn it," I growl, slamming my hand on the kitchen table. Why had I been making coffee in the first place?

"You all right in there?" I can hear John walking toward the kitchen. "Did you burn yourself?"

"No, no. I'm fine. Just disappointed you stopped. For a few seconds there, I felt like I had a backstage pass."

"Well, you did, and you will when you listen to the Wheelhouse Café over the radio too."

"The Baton Rouge lady you're singing about—who is she?"

"I wrote that song to remember someone who got me through some dark days."

"Lucky you," I say, raising an eyebrow, "or maybe I should say lucky her?" I look down and then right back up into John's eyes. "I want to apologize for letting the Wheelhouse Café cat out of the bag with Chase. I got caught up in the moment and forgot. I really do try to be vault-like on the secret front."

"Vault-like, huh?" John is nodding with a ridiculous grin.

"Hey, I'm being serious here." I give him a little push. "You've been keeping it under wraps for a long time, and I feel really bad."

"Listen, I only keep it quiet because tying up a radio channel isn't on the list of Coast Guard–approved activities. It's not because I'm shy."

"Oh," I say. "Is that so? Hmm . . ."

"And, there's something about being under cover that appeals to my rogue spirit."

"I can only imagine," I say, feeling better now.

"It's mysterious. Like Meow Man."

"Meow Man?" I ask.

"The guy tags all sorts of things up and down the Eastern Seaboard. He draws the outline of a cat's head and then writes *Meow Man was here* next to it."

"What sorts of things?"

"Oh, you'll see *Meow Man* on bridges, tanks, barge hulls."

"And Meow Man is . . . you?" My eyes widen.

"No," John says. "I have a theory, though I'm not sure I could prove it. Or, that I'd want to. What I'm trying to say is a little mystery goes a long way when you're living on a tug. Keeps things interesting."

"Same thing could be said for us landlubbers," I say.

"Landlubbers?" John coughs his way into a laugh.

"Is my lingo not cool enough for you, Captain John?" I ask, unable to suppress a smile. I take a half step back as he moves toward me.

"Arden," he says, getting even closer, "first, I'm going to kiss you. Then, I'm going to make you the best cup of coffee you've ever had."

I follow John's play-by-play with, "First, I'm going to tell you that you're a mind reader. And then, I'm going to shut up so you can kiss me."

There's a buzz in the air, soft and electric. I feel like I'm skipping rocks across the still surface of the bay, relishing every ripple.

John presses against me, sliding his hands—those hands –behind my head. Our lips touch briefly, and then he kisses my left cheek. My nose. My right eyelid. My chin. When he kisses around my lips, I part them a little, an invitation.

And then the phone rings. We jump away from each other. "Is this where one of us is supposed to say *Saved by the bell*, or something like that?" he asks, leaning back to sit on the top of my desk.

"Yeah, something like that," I say, my heart still ricocheting as I pick up the phone. "Hello?" It's Chase. Checking in. "Hey, Chase. Yes, everything's fine here. Radio's all set up and ready to go. Now we're having some lunch. And coffee. Coffee too." I'm talking too much—too fast and too much. Maybe I am my mother's daughter after all. "OK, see you at three thirty."

Usually, I'd be three steps ahead of myself, trying to map out what's next, but I'm unable to be anywhere other than right here. I hang up, turning to look at John. "Gotta admire his sixth sense," he says.

I move back into John's arms and lay my head on his chest, glad to feel his heart is quick-stepping too. "You know, I'm actually looking forward to missing you for a few days," I say.

"Ah, the lady is not immune to tugboat syndrome after all. She's longing to allow sea time to heighten normally mundane experiences, erase giant relationship problems, and create a pervasive sense of false happiness."

"That's your diagnosis?" I ask. "Can't say I agree. Kissing you was anything but mundane. I *do* like the idea of having it physically impossible for us to move on to anything else because you'll be gone for two weeks."

"Not *impossible*," he says. "You could stow away."

"You'll already have one stowaway on board. I'd say that's enough to handle for one trip."

He gives me a long embrace and a soft kiss on the lips. John looks down at his watch. "It's one already. I'll have that cup of coffee and head back to my place to pack."

"Sounds good," I say. "Want to take a sandwich too?" He nods.

We're both quiet for a while, and I've never been so aware of making a sandwich before—the texture of the bread, the tart smell of the pickle, the smooth Swiss and thin, light pink slices of ham. I hand it to John as he takes a final swig of coffee.

"Thanks," he says. "See you at three thirty. Try not to get lost. And don't forget Charlie's coming by to put up that antenna. Will you let Murray know?"

"Aye, aye, Captain," I say. "See you soon."

"Nice guitar," he says, motioning toward that corner of the room as he opens the door."

"Glad you spotted it so your music could help us skip over all the *blah blah blah*."

"Anyone ever tell you you're quite the wordsmith?"

I mouth *blah blah blah*, cocking my head to one side. John walks into the hallway, shaking his head.

When the door clicks shut, I stand motionless in the kitchen doorway. My place seems different, warmer and full of anticipation. I pour a cup of coffee and stir in a splash of milk. Then I go over to the desk and put my hand on the radio.

Chapter Fourteen: John

Wednesday, May 18, 1994

Is it really only yesterday that Arden had invited me to the gallery opening? I barely allowed myself to hope I might get to know her better when feelings I didn't have time for knocked me over, and now I had a whole new cast of characters thrust into my life.

There's no turning back. I'm almost more concerned about how things are accelerating with Arden than I am about having Garrett as my sidekick at sea. I'm counting on the way salty air and distance helps me make sense of things, and part of me is hoping I'm just caught up in a moment. The last thing I want to do is disappoint someone Billy cared about, and I can't imagine things turning out any other way.

Packing has become a reflex. I roll my clothes into a long canvas duffle, and after too many last-minute dashes for toothpaste or shampoo, I've gotten into the habit of refilling my Dopp kit right when I get home.

I give my apartment a last look. My fireplace is too clean, and I realize I haven't built a fire since Christmas. I used to burn one every night, more for the sound of the flames than for their warmth. I always add driftwood to the mix. Salt water–soaked wood crackles with more intensity and sends up green- and blue-laced flames.

When I was in high school, we started watching the Yule log on television during the holidays. Mom always wanted a fireplace, and we'd talked about getting one every year—where we'd put it, should we get a wood stove instead—but when it never materialized, the Yule log became our makeshift substitute. I looked forward to the mesmerizing sight and sound of that virtual fire until one of my *Reality Bites* girlfriends made me feel like a stupid ass when she told me it was just a single, repetitive, fifteen-second frame.

Before I lug my bag into the elevator, I knock on my neighbor's door. "Hello!" I shout. "It's John."

Mrs. Noonaby opens the door, holding a fat calico cat in her arms. "Well hello, Captain," she says. "Time for a cup of tea?"

"I wish, but no time for tea today. Just want you to know I'm on my way out. Be back in two weeks."

"Oh," she says, not trying to hide her disappointment. "Well, if you must leave, then leave you must. You know you can count on me to stand a most vigilant watch while you're gone."

"Of this I can be sure. Be good to yourself, will you? Let Carlisle know if you need anything."

"Carlisle is a curmudgeon." She crunches up her nose.

"C'mon, he's not so bad," I say, though I agree that our neighbor is much grumpier than he needs to be. "And if there's an emergency . . ."

"If there's an emergency, I'll call the NYPD or the FDNY," she says firmly. "What would Carlisle do, anyway? I'm surprised he can take care of himself, let alone think of anyone else."

"Point well taken," I say. Martha sends me off with a wink. Even though we don't see each other every day, I know I'm one of the few constants in her life, someone who knows her favorite color (moss green) and what she likes to eat for lunch (bologna—Boar's Head only—on whole wheat with little pickles and onions).

It's not until I start walking toward the parking garage to get my truck that it really sinks in—I'm about twenty minutes away from diving headfirst into this scheme. Once we leave the dock, there won't be any turning back. Should I be more worried? Not having any young children in my life, I have no idea what I'm in for.

Filling the hours, how tough can it really be? Garrett and I can play cards. Is there really any harm in an eight-year-old learning every poker variation known to man? I can teach him the constellations and give him guitar lessons. Arden said she's bringing a stack of books. I might even dredge up a few of the stories my Uncle Geoffrey used to tell me about Bruno the giant grasshopper. I laugh aloud realizing I haven't thought of Uncle Gee-off or the Bruno stories in years. I used to beg for them. I was the lead character, and Bruno was my faithful sidekick. The plot was always the same—the two of us working our way in and out of trouble, somehow managing to help people and learn valuable lessons along the way.

I'll have to tell the guys to lay off the language and endless rounds of *Would Ya?* this trip. Usually, they'll play an ongoing game where someone says the name of a beautiful celebrity or holds up a glossy magazine photo of a naked goddess and asks, *Would Ya?* You'd be surprised how discriminating a bunch of horny, badly groomed, sometimes downright ugly men can be.

I hope the radio will be a comfort to Garrett and that talking to his family doesn't make him feel disconnected. I never like being reminded that I'm floating around on the outskirts of civilization while life goes on without me, but talking on the radio can also transform a day at sea.

Ronnie is the perfect example. She used to work for VTS—Vessel Traffic Services—and never failed to evoke a unanimous *yes* in *Would ya?* Her voice was so thick and smooth that it was trance inducing. We all had our theories—OK, fantasies–about Ronnie. For a solid two years, we'd speculated on what she looked like, what she was wearing or not wearing, what she liked to do when she wasn't on the radio, or even if her name was really Ronnie.

My version? Something like this: Ronnie was a former volleyball ace with broad shoulders and rippling muscles. She wore her hair wrapped up in a tight bun at work, but the rest of the time it fell around her shoulders. Ronnie would silence the room when she walked in—bright eyes, curves, and a killer smile. Her sense of humor was rough around the edges. And of course, she loved spending long afternoons in bed finding ways to amuse herself and whoever was lucky enough to end up there with her. I laugh aloud again remembering how much time and energy we all devoted to "imagining Ronnie."

One of the captains, Jimmy MacDermott, finally worked up the nerve to ask her out. We all thought she'd turn him down, but when she jumped at the opportunity, it was all we could do to suppress our jealousy and curiosity waiting for his Ronnie report. Me? I would've taken one for the team out of respect for time invested and fantasies crafted. Unfortunately for us, Jimmy Mac was an honest man and shattered our visions of Ronnie with a few choice descriptive words—buckteeth and body odor.

I get to the *Alanna Rose* at three to see if it's going to be my lucky day, or if I should brace myself for a trip from hell. I find Marakesh and Joe Jo James clanking around down below. Little Hal is on deck, checking the lines. Benny, the new guy, is unloading groceries in the galley, humming, "This Little Light of Mine." Only Darryl is missing, and he might not show up anyway. I decide to wait for Garrett's arrival to tell everyone about our stowaway. No need to give anyone time to ask questions or make phone calls.

Everyone descends on the dock at once. Or I should say they arrived simultaneously, but not together. Arden comes from one direction, lugging three big shopping bags. Garrett's posse tumbles out of a cab. Chase pays the driver as Garrett, flanked by his mom and grandmother, carries his own bags, one small duffel and a backpack. I watch him turn his head from one to the other as they try to talk to him at once. He breaks into a run when he notices me. "Captain John! I'm ready to cast off!"

"Good to hear my chief mate's ready to roll."

"Roll?" he asks with a scrunched up face. "Ohhh, you mean *roll on the waves* roll."

"I mean rock 'n roll, but I like the way you think. Nice."

Everyone else catches up then, surrounding us. "All right, Captain John," Marva says. "Garrett's packed up. Where's the tugboat?"

I don't know how she could miss the 135 feet of steel tied up next to us. It's not until I say, "She's right here. Let me introduce you to the Tug

Alanna Rose," that I realize they seem surprised to see a 6,000 horsepower tug. "Why do I get the feeling you were expecting Little Toot?" I ask.

"She is *some* tug, Captain Raymond," Chase says as he takes Garrett's bags from him.

"You can say that again." Macy is clearly impressed.

"When will you be able to call us on the radio?" Marva asks.

"How about we check in with you around dinnertime? After that, I can't be sure. We won't always be within range."

Marva keeps crossing and uncrossing her arms, but Macy remains steady. As Garrett walks toward the *Alanna Rose,* I see Macy turn to Chase. "We can't be sending Garrett out to sea every single time Levi threatens to show up. We really need to figure this out while he's gone."

Chase takes her hand. "We will. That's what this is all about, Macy. Keeping everyone safe while we figure this out."

Arden is staring off into space, still holding all her bags. "Let me give you a hand with those," I say.

She snaps to, almost like she's forgotten about them. "Thanks. Man, I really zoned out. Must be the fresh air." My hand brushes against hers as I take the bags. I had no idea how badly I'd want to touch her, and how difficult it would be to keep my hands to myself.

"What'd you buy the kid, a ton of bricks?" I ask, peering into one of the bags.

"Books, mostly, but some games, too," Arden says. "And puzzles. I got a little carried away, but fourteen days is a long time. You'll thank me later."

"I'll thank you now," I say, marveling at how her eyes light up when I say, "Thank you."

Chase is still talking to Macy. It doesn't seem like he's picked up on a shift between Arden and me, and I don't know if that's good or bad. Two weeks is going to give him plenty of time to try to get closer to Arden. I can tell I'm not even on his radar as a potential threat. I don't think he discounts me for any reason other than he can't comprehend not getting something he sets his sights on.

That's when I see Darryl hobbling toward us, visibly picking up his pace when he spots me. I wave as he passes by. "Time to meet the crew," I say.

"All of us?" Macy asks.

"All of you," I reply.

Garrett jumps from dock to deck with confidence. Then Arden hops on as Chase and I help Marva and Macy. The tugboat is already having its usual effect on its new acquaintances. Everyone seems starry-eyed.

Little Hal is still nearby, and I ask him to call into the galley and then down into the engine room. By the time the crew gathers on deck, I decide to make my spiel even shorter and sweeter. "I've got some introductions to make," I say. "We've got a special passenger aboard this trip. Garrett?" Garrett scurries over to stand next to me. "Garrett is going to be my chief mate. This is his mom, Marva, his grandmother, Macy, and his good friends, Chase and Arden."

Marakesh winks at Macy and says, "Grandma? You gotta be kidding me." He elbows Garrett and says, "Lucky you, hitting the gene pool jackpot."

I decide to take the introduction one step further. "Why don't you all head into the galley while I get the crew in motion?" I direct this to Chase. "I'll meet you there for a quick tour before we leave."

Once Garrett and his crew are out of earshot I say, "The kid's in danger. His dad's coming to town looking to kidnap him and has threatened to hurt his mom and grandmother. We'll be keeping Garrett safe while everyone who cares about him figures out the best way to deal with the asshole."

I know that making them feel like they're on the inside and involved in keeping Garrett safe is a good idea, and they react as I suspected they would—with a rumble of genuine support. *We'll keep it on the down low. Happy to have him aboard. Poor kid. My dad was an asshole too.*

Then it's time for a twenty-second tour. I walk into the galley and say, "This is the galley. Not to be called a kitchen, mind you." Garrett and I exchange winks, and Arden doesn't take her eyes off me.

Chapter Fifteen: Arden

Wednesday, May 18, 1994

Sometimes I think it's a good thing there's no time to say things you think you want to say. John is so right about tugboat syndrome. There's something about knowing he's going to be away that's heightening the intensity of my feelings. I want to wrap my arms around him. I want to kiss him again. I want to be alone with him for a few seconds just to hear him say my name.

Our good-bye is quick and impersonal. There's so much going on, and the focus is where it should be—on Garrett. There are brief hugs all around. John and I come together in more of a sideways squeeze than a full-on hug, and we don't make eye contact. I feel light-headed when I step down to the dock.

Garrett waves wildly from the bow. Marva and Macy stand on the dock, blowing and throwing kisses. There aren't any tears until the boat starts pulling away. That's when Marva turns her back to the water, and they start to flow. "I'm so grateful that he'll be fine with John, but I just can't forgive myself for creating a life where my kid can't even be safe in his own home." She cries harder, almost snorting, and her non–soap opera cry is a testament to the ties that bind us.

Chase puts his finger under her chin, forcing her to look up. "Enough of that. You're a great mom," he says. "Garrett is going to be safe, and so are you. C'mon, let's get to Arden's and give that radio a try."

We wait for a cab in silence, and just when I begin to wonder if taxi traffic exists here, one approaches. We zip toward my apartment, Chase up front listening to the driver talk about his daughter's senior thesis and me squeezed in between a silent Marva and Aunt Macy.

Everything rolls from there. When we arrive at my place, Murray tells us John's friend has been there, and the antenna is all set. Good news. We file into my apartment, and I keep focusing on the moment at hand to avoid looking at the guitar John perched back in the corner.

"*This* is the radio," I say when we finally make it to my desk. "And here's how it works." I turn to Channel 68 and pick up the mic. "This is Arden McHale to the *Alanna Rose*." The radio sputters, but no answer from John.

"Don't you have a handle?" Chase jokes.

"I'm not a trucker. But if I did have one, it would be Mermaid. Definitely."

"Very fitting," he says.

"Captain John Raymond, this is Arden. Do you read me?"

His response follows as soon as I release the mic. "The *Alanna Rose* to the *Arden McHale*. Over."

"Sounds like I'm standing right next to you," I reply, hoping the words I *wish* remained inside my head instead of actually leaving my lips. "Where are you?"

"Just picked up a loaded oil barge and we'll be northbound up the Hudson shortly." There was a slight pause, and then we hear Garrett. "Arden, it's me!"

"Hi, there," I answer. "Your mom's right here."

Even though I've only been given a much-abbreviated VHF Marine Radio course, I know we'll have to keep our conversations short and sweet. John told me lots of people could listen in, and I know that even though John has us using one of the least popular channels, hearing a child's voice would raise a red flag.

"I love you, baby," Marva says. "We all miss you already but know you're going to have so much fun."

"You'll see me soon, Mom," he answers. "And I love you too, but I need to get back to work now."

Marva isn't crying anymore, but she's not smiling either. She holds the mic in both hands, staring at it. "You do that. I'll talk to you soon. Grandma Macy sends a hug."

I take the mic back. "Over and out, Captain Raymond," I say.

"You can just say, 'Over,' next time. The 'and out' isn't necessary."

"Thanks for the tip, *Captain*," I say, "I'll talk to you soon."

"Yes, soon," he answers. "Over."

I don't like the whole *over* scenario. *Over and out* is buoyant and jaunty. *Over* just seems—well, *over*.

"Arden. Earth to Arden." Chase only manages to get my attention when he taps his fist lightly on the side of my head. "Still with us?"

"Oh, I'm here, all right," I say. "Just a little tired and zoned out."

"I'm bringing these ladies home to get some things and figure out where they're staying. Want to grab dinner later?"

I see Aunt Macy shoot me an expectant look.

"Sounds great, but I'm really beat, Chase. How about you call me in a couple of hours? I may feel like a new woman by then."

I can tell my answer surprises him, and he gives me a curt, "I'll talk to you later," as he heads out with Marva and Aunt Macy. I'm so grateful to be alone that I don't give his moodiness any more thought. We're all beat.

I crumple onto the couch; the apartment is quiet except for its usual hum. I don't want to doze off, so I move over to the desk. I've decided to leave the radio on all the time, just in case. And now I can't bear to take my eyes off it, like I might miss John appearing right in front of me if I look away.

Then I hear him. John's voice is coming through the radio as though I've summoned it. He's singing about a Long Island sailor on the Jersey Shore. I don't recognize the song and figure it must be one of his originals. His singing voice doesn't sound anything like his speaking voice. It's deeper and rougher around the edges. Every once in a while, I hear a shuffling sound and can almost see Garrett shifting in his seat or getting up to walk around the wheelhouse.

I close my eyes and imagine standing on the bow of the tug, watching the horizon squeeze sunlight out of the evening sky, a steadfast squeegee making room for a canvas of stars. I see myself leaning back onto John, his arms around me, and his voice low and sweet in my ear. I look at the guitar in the corner and think about sitting on the floor next to John while he writes a new song.

"Arden, are you there?"

John's voice startles me. I sit up and applaud wildly even though I know John can't hear me.

"I'm just clapping with wild abandon," I say into the mic.

"I thought I lost you there."

"You did lose me. That song is so beautiful. It took me away."

"That bad, huh?"

"Billy was right, you know." I pause, too greedy to offer any more encouragement. "I demand an encore."

"Not tonight. Duty calls." For the first time in our conversation, I remember John isn't going to be around for a while and feel the rush of time running out.

"Can we talk later?" Why does my voice have to sound so tinny?

"Probably not. We'll be back in the harbor soon, though. Maybe even by tomorrow. We'll see how it goes."

We'll see how it goes. If my inability to move away from the radio is any indication, I know exactly how it's going to go. "OK, great," is what I say. "Thanks for the song."

What the hell is going on with me? First swim of the season notwithstanding, I'm someone who needs to test the waters before I jump into anything. And now I'm immersed in something I don't understand. Me, the girl who doesn't believe in love at first sight and has even made a habit of having lust wait its turn.

The phone rings. Maybe it's Chase? Meeting him sounds like a much better idea now that I don't want to think about how I feel about John or where Levi is or how I'm going to be dodging pangs of missing Billy for the rest of my life. I need a drink.

Chapter Sixteen: John

Wednesday, May 18, 1994

"So, here we are," I say, placing my guitar back in its case. "You and me and the sea." Garrett is quiet, staring out the expansive wheelhouse windows. I can't tell if he's mesmerized, terrified, or both. "Want a snack before bed?" I ask. "It's almost nine, and you didn't really eat much for dinner."

"Do tugboat people eat peanut butter?" he asks. I nod. "Then I'd like an open-faced peanut butter sandwich, please."

"Right on," I say. "We're going to the galley, Little Hal."

He touches the tip of his Mets cap, keeping his eyes on the Hudson.

Garrett approaches the narrow metal staircase with confidence. His hand slides down the banister as he puts one foot in front of the other. He hops off the bottom step onto the deck. "Could I make the sandwich?" he asks. "Please. I have a special technique."

I don't know what impressed me more—his use of the word technique or his self-sufficiency. "Of course," I answer. "I have a lot to learn in the peanut butter sandwich department."

When we get to the galley, Benny is sitting at the table playing solitaire. "Hey there," he says. "Welcome aboard." Garrett shakes his hand vigorously and asks, "Would you like a peanut butter sandwich?" It's in this moment that I'm sure Garrett will be OK—not just for these two weeks, but also beyond that, when life is still throwing curveballs at him. The kid has good instincts, and he knows how to connect with people.

"I haven't had a peanut butter sandwich in about twenty years," Benny says. "I'd love one with an ice cold glass of milk."

"Coming right up!" Garrett slaps the table with enthusiasm. "Captain John, how about you?"

"I wouldn't miss it. Peanut butter's in the cabinet next to the fridge, bread on top, silverware in the wooden box by the sink. See the plates there on the shelf?"

Garrett is already in motion, so I sit down across from Benny. We've worked together on and off for years, and I still don't know much about him. I do know he came up from Louisiana during the strike in 1987, and that he still speaks slowly and musically. He likes to carve bars of soap into jungle animals, and he drinks lots and lots of green tea.

Garrett whistles as he moves around the galley with purpose.

Benny pipes right up. "Hey kid, since you're the chief mate, I gotta fill you in something, sailor to sailor. Whistling on a boat is bad luck."

"Bad luck? Why?" Garrett asks.

"Superstition." Benny says. "Sailors have a long-held belief that whistling on board a ship will whistle up a storm."

"That's sounds too crazy to be true," Garrett says.

"Maybe so, but the last place you want to tempt fate is at sea. I can tell you about a lotta superstitions on this trip. We've got time."

Garrett pops the bread into the toaster, getting right into his peanut butter groove. "This is my secret to the perfect peanut butter sandwich," he says, standing up a bit taller. "The bread isn't *totally* toasted, just warm enough to melt the peanut butter a little bit."

"Aha," Benny says. "Ingenious. When did you get to be such a gourmet, anyway?"

"Grandma Macy is teaching me everything she knows," Garrett says. "We cook dinner for my mom every night, and we make the best after-school snacks."

"I never knew either of my grandmothers," Benny says. "You're a lucky boy."

Garrett looks surprised. "I'm sorry, Benny."

"That's OK, kid. I've survived all right. My mom's mother already passed on by the time I was born, and I never met my father or his family."

"I don't know my father very well either," Garrett admits, taking the first two slices out of the toaster and replacing them with two more. "He lives in California or Iowa or someplace like that. And he drives trucks all over the world. Even to Alaska and Canada."

"Wow," Benny says, without glancing at me. "Cool."

"I guess," Garrett says. "He doesn't like me very much."

I decide to intervene, even though I've promised myself to steer clear of any attempts at child psychology. "Garrett. That's not true."

"How do you know, Captain John? My dad says mean things to me. And he hurts Mom and Grandma too. If he likes me, why would he hurt us?" Garrett turns to place the first sandwich in front of Benny who nods a *thank you* and starts eating.

"I don't know your dad, but I do know that sometimes grown-ups do things that don't make sense for reasons even they don't understand," I say. "You're a great kid with a great mom and grandma who love you like crazy. And your dad loves you too, even though he has other things going on that may make him act like a jerk sometimes."

"I don't know," Garrett says, taking out the second round of slices and putting in the final two. "I do know I don't like it when he calls."

"I hear you, Chef Garrett," Benny says. "You just keep on keeping it real, 'cause you're one cool cat."

Garrett places my sandwich in front of me and stands by the toaster waiting for his to pop up. He taps his fingers on the cutting board.

I watch him, thinking about what my life was like when I was his age. My father was always at his hardware store, and I spent a lot of time there too. I would sweep the floor, talk to customers, and just hang around. I never heard my father raise his voice, not to me or anyone else. It occurred to me that an unsettling realization had just been introduced to Garrett's world—that sometimes the people who are supposed to love you the most don't always know how.

"All set, Captain John," Garrett says, wrapping his sandwich in a paper towel. "Can I eat this in bed?"

"No," I answer. Benny chuckles, and Garrett asks why. "Because we don't have beds on boats. You can eat your sandwich in your rack, though."

He looks at me quizzically. "My rack?"

"That's where you're sleeping. You'll see. Let's go."

Once he climbs in, Garrett clicks on the little reading lamp above his head. "I'm going to eat this while I read some books," he says.

"You can read?" I ask.

"Well, some words, and I can figure the rest out from the pictures, or I just use my imagination. Sometimes I think the stories I make up are better anyway."

"Does someone usually tell you a bedtime story? Anything like that?" In all the frenzy, we hadn't touched on Garrett's nighttime routine.

"Sometimes, but I don't need a story. I do need to brush my teeth when I've finished this sandwich though, so I'll be getting up to do that."

"Thanks for remembering. I'm heading back up to the wheelhouse. You know where to find me. And remember, you can go from your room to the head or up to the wheelhouse, but do not under any circumstances go out on deck by yourself."

"The head—that's the bathroom, right?" he asks.

"You got it."

"Good night, Captain John," he puts his hand out for a low five.

"'Night, Garrett. Good to have you aboard. And thanks for the best peanut butter sandwich ever."

"You're welcome." He's already munching on half a sandwich while looking down at the book in his hand.

I go topside to the wheelhouse, relieved that this day is almost over. Little Hal heads down without asking me any questions, leaving me alone to navigate up the Hudson. It's especially dark along this stretch, so dark that sometimes the glowing Amtrak looks meteor-like, hurtling it's way from Albany to New York.

The stars compete for my attention, and I think about teaching Garrett how to find constellations so he can experience the comfort that comes with getting to know the immense night sky.

Chapter Seventeen: Arden

Wednesday, May 18, 1994

A power nap and shower don't do much to revive me from cramming what feels like an entire week into twenty-four hours. I am feeling more indecisive though, and I change clothes three times before leaving to meet Chase. My linen blouse turns me into a giant wrinkle, and my jeans make me question why they're my favorites. Finally, I settle on a hot pink twin set and sheer layered skirt. Better.

When I spoke to Chase on the phone, I could hear the excitement in his voice, even though he tried to act all *did we talk about meeting for dinner?* I tell myself not to feel guilty that my second wind is fueled by a sudden and irrepressible need to be distracted from my inability to get Billy's disappearance, Levi's looming arrival, and John and his tugboat serenade out of my head. Sure, there are other, less-complicated diversions at my disposal—catching a movie, plowing through the pile of work on my desk, or maybe wrangling up plans with someone on my increasingly short list of friends unafraid to go out on a Wednesday night. But I am both sleep-deprived and a creature of habit, so of course I choose the admirer waiting in the wings.

When I get to Regional Thai, I'm not surprised to find the perpetually early Chase already camped out at an outside table. I exhale into the familiarity of the moment. "Will I ever beat you to the scene?" I ask. "I used to consider myself punctual."

"There's always a chance my cab will get a flat or I'll get lost. Otherwise, no. I'm chronically early. Even when I think I'm running late, I end up arriving on time."

Our table is on the corner of the small patio area, my chair back to back with someone eating at the Mexican restaurant next door. I admire the unobstructed view of my all-time favorite graffiti declaration emblazoned on the building across the street—*Old Lady Loves Neckface*.

We're both soaked in our surroundings, and I tune into the soundtrack of street traffic and eighties music, a Regional Thai staple. "Boy George," I say. "A favorite of yours, am I right?"

"Actually, I've always considered myself to be more of an Oingo Boingo kind of guy."

"Hmm . . . never would have guessed." Already, it's easy to be here. I don't feel the need to impress Chase.

"So, any word from Ahab and Queequeg?" he asks, opening his menu.

"As a matter of fact, yes. John and Garrett did call just as I was walking out the door."

"Really? So soon?" I sense a twang of tension.

"Garrett sounds great," I continue. "Right at home. And John's keeping him occupied with the guitar."

"Garrett is playing the guitar?" Chase asks.

"No, John is. But Garrett loves it. And I imagine there'll be lessons at some point. Those boys have a lot of time on their hands."

"I'm glad they're doing well. Marva and Macy seem to be in good spirits. Steady. We want to meet tomorrow night to talk about a plan."

"A plan, right." I sigh and watch a dog walker untangling himself from a web of leashes. "That is the point of all this."

"Exactly," Chase says. "I'm so tired right now, I can't think straight. In fact, I'm not thinking at all."

"I'm on autopilot too. Exhausted."

My favorite waiter brings us two short glasses of tap water, takes our orders, and sashays back inside. "I wonder if your next bright idea can top the one that has Garrett heading up the Hudson on a tugboat right now?"

"Who knows what crazy scheme I'll dream up next?" I lift my water glass to clink his as our cocktails arrive.

"I do think the only real solution is to file a report. If Macy and Marva won't go to the police, there must be some agency that can help."

"I've urged them to get a restraining order so there's something official for Levi to violate, but even now I think they'll want to avoid the police," I say. "Part of their resistance is fear-based, but I think most of it has to do with a sense of failure—like somehow they've failed as a family if they have to turn to the police to intervene in their lives."

The waiter places two plates of Pad Thai in front of us, and I order another round of drinks.

"Levi is not going to stop unless he's stopped," Chase says, twirling noodles around his fork. I always make a mental note of whether or not someone uses chopsticks. "And the older Garrett gets, the harder this whole situation will become."

"In some ways," I agree. "But in others, I feel like the more time we buy Garrett, the more self-esteem and confidence he'll develop. He'll be able to handle more."

"I don't know, Arden. Don't you feel a sense of urgency? I mean for all we know, Levi's already here, and if he's not, he will be soon. Garrett's not developing confidence if he's worried about being safe. And since Levi already hurt Macy and Marva in front of him, we have to assume his violence will escalate."

"I can't even imagine someone hurting Garrett," I bite my lower lip and stare at the table.

"No one's going to hurt Garrett." He puts his hand over mine and squeezes it. "Hey, the good news is we're all in this together. And we're going to work it out. You have to trust in that."

"I do, I do," I say. Chase's focus goes from looking at me to *looking* at me. I don't take my eyes off his, not because I'm lost in them, but because I've slipped into thinking about John and how he would feel about me having this intense moment with Chase. I know how I'd feel if John was having dinner with a woman who was trying to get closer to him. Chase leans in to brush his lips against mine, mistaking my returned gaze for an invitation.

My eyes are closed, and I need to think fast. What expression do I wear when I open them? I didn't want to kiss Chase. Maybe I wasn't sure about that a few hours ago when I was determined to push John out of my head, but I was sure now.

A tear rolls down my right cheek. "Did I just move you to tears?" Chase asks playfully. Even as I scramble to think of how to shift back into friendship mode, I know it's already too late. His eagerness makes me wish I hadn't thought this was a good idea.

"Sorry about that," I say, brushing the tear away. "I was . . . um, I was, thinking about Billy."

"We just kissed, and you're thinking about Billy?"

"*You* kissed *me*." I don't give Chase a chance to dispute the facts "I was telling you the truth when I said I wasn't in love with Billy. I don't know what else to say." Our conversation at yesterday's midmorning cocktail party seems a million miles away.

"The fact that you have to think about what to say says it all." He pushes back his plate.

That's when exhaustion sets in. I can't find the energy for this conversation or to finish my dinner. I can't even imagine hailing a cab home. All I want to do is slide beneath my sheets and rest my head on a cool pillow.

"You're tired," I say. "I'm tired. In fact, I'm more exhausted than I can ever remember being. This isn't the time to have a conversation about feelings."

"That's just it, Arden. There shouldn't even have to be a conversation. If you really want to be with someone, the timing is never off, no matter how exhausted or scared or distracted you may be."

"Maybe so. I don't know, Chase, and I'm sorry for not knowing. I'm sorry for everything. I think I should just head home."

"Yeah, you're right. That's probably a good idea."

When I reach into my bag for my wallet, he barks, "Just let me get it, would you? I mean, honestly."

"Thank you," I say, not responding to his tone.

"You're welcome. But I can't say I understand. I mean, I really thought we were on the same page. We were clicking." He finally looks up, and my expression must be what dissuades him from continuing. "Good night, Arden."

"About tomorrow night . . ." I start, almost wincing when I remember we'll be in plan mode together.

He just shakes his head and says, "I'll be there."

I squeeze through the maze of chairs and decide to walk up a block before crossing over to Sixth Avenue for a cab. I don't want to stand on the corner of 22nd and Seventh waiting for the light to turn, wondering if Chase is watching me leave. Part of me believes him. If you want to be with someone, there's no such thing as bad timing.

The city pulses with possibility. There are millions of people here, sometimes colliding and connecting, sometimes crossing paths and moving on. I think of Aunt Macy's insightful kitchen observation and realize that my universe has shifted in a matter of hours—one admirer being flung out of my orbit, and the other making me spin out of control.

Chapter Eighteen: John

Thursday, May 19, 1994

I haven't always been a morning person, but now I find myself anticipating the end of midwatch, knowing that means I'll have a front-row seat for daybreak. Some mornings erupt with fiery impatience, while others seep in with muted restraint.

"Good morning!" Garrett chirps, bounding into the galley. "What time is it?"

"About seven thirty."

"Wow! Slept in. Must be the salty air," he says, taking a deep breath in through his nose and then shifting his weight from one foot to another. "And the way this boat rocks. At first I didn't like it. You like it?"

I nodded. "Sometimes when I get home, I have a hard time falling asleep without it."

"Are you off watch now?" Garrett asks, visibly pleased with himself for using the word *watch*.

"Off till about eleven thirty."

"So you probably need to sleep, right?"

"I'll catch a nap soon. Let's get you some breakfast first."

"Cereal's good," Garrett says. "Do tugboats have cereal?"

"*This* tugboat has cereal," I say, with a broad gesture toward a bright row of cereal boxes.

"Wow! You've got my favorites. All of 'em." He pulls down the Fruit Loops and finishes his bowl with just a few scoops.

"Little Hal's in the wheelhouse," I say. "Why don't we get you set up with some books and blocks up there? When I wake up, we can do a puzzle before my watch."

"Great," he says. "I have a freaky jellyfish one that you're gonna love." I have to give it to the kid. He makes going with the flow seem effortless.

"Where are we, anyway?" he asks.

"We're in Tarrytown, waiting to head back down the river."

"Already? That was fast." Garrett cocks his head and looks at me. "That *was* fast, right?"

"Yes, it was. We made good time while you were far away in dreamland. And before you know it, we'll be steaming back to New York Harbor. Just waiting for our orders. Why don't you change out of your pajamas and meet me in the wheelhouse?"

I go up to talk to Little Hal about hanging with Garrett. I hoped he wouldn't mind the company. I'd somehow forgotten that even I need to sleep sometimes. Every time I think about Garrett wandering around unsupervised, I shiver. I don't even know if the kid can swim. Even though he wears a life jacket on deck, the thought of him going overboard makes me nauseous.

Little Hal doesn't flinch at the idea of having a temporary sidekick. Within minutes, Garrett shows up in the wheelhouse hauling his fully loaded backpack. *Arden.* The image of her stuffing his bag with coloring books and Go Fish cards makes me ache. It's an intoxicating, aggravating smackdown, proving just how much I need these two weeks to get a grip.

Garrett yanks on my shirt, breathless. "Captain John, Little Hal says he's going to let me steer. Can you believe it?! I'm gonna *drive . . . the . . . tug!*" He bounces up and down a few more times before collapsing on the wheelhouse floor.

I squat down to tap him on the shoulder. "For the next few hours, whatever Little Hal says goes. Got it? C'mon, time to get up and get to work." Garrett pulls himself together and stands at attention. "I'm hitting the rack. You two have fun. Thanks again, Hal."

"I should be thanking you," Little Hal says. "It gets lonely up here. Not to mention we're all better off with someone who can actually see at the helm."

I hear Garrett ask, "What's the helm again? Captain John told me, but I can't remember . . ."

The closer I get to my rack, the more I can feel how long my body and mind have been running on empty. I can't even remember the last time I slept—was it during those few hours between leaving the gallery and when Arden called?

When my head hits the pillow, I'm startled by the image of Chase, like he's a precursor to a dream. Did Arden see him last night? In the very first days Meredith and I were together, I'd done a lot of wondering about what was going on while I was gone, mostly because I'd figured out early on with Meredith—she craved attention and soaked it up from anyone who'd give it to her. When I called her from some crappy dockside pay phone, my competitive nature would shift into overdrive if she didn't answer.

Today, exhaustion is on my side. The whirl of thoughts stops once I close my eyes. Garrett is safe, and the smell of Arden's shampoo and the memory of her soft lips are still in my head.

* * *

"Captain John," Garrett whispers in my ear. "It's time to wake up. I'm your human alarm clock."

I open my eyes to find Garrett's face a few inches from mine. "Well, hello there. And, what time *is* it, human alarm clock?"

"It's coffee time!" he cheers. "And maybe soup and grilled cheese time too?"

"I like the sound of that. Did you put Little Hal to work in the galley?"

"Oh, no. Soup's from a can, and grilled cheese happens to be another one of my specialties."

"You'd better be careful," I say as my feet hit the deck. "We might need to hire you full time if you keep dazzling us with your culinary skills."

"My what?" he asks, leading the way to the galley.

"Your ability to cook better than any of us. You've got skills."

"No biggie," Garrett says.

Before stepping into the galley, I take a look around. We had made quite a bit of headway while I slept and are approaching New York Harbor.

"Garrett, I'm going to take a rain check on lunch in the galley," I say. "Maybe you could bring a sandwich up to the wheelhouse for me?"

"Roger that," he says.

"Are you allowed to use the stove without grown-ups around?"

"Not when I'm alone, but I'm not alone on the tug, am I? Sometimes Grandma Macy goes down to the laundry room when we're making dinner together, so that's kinda like you being in the wheelhouse. I can handle it."

I decide to believe him and give him a wink of confidence on my way up to the wheelhouse. I have a few minutes to burn before I relieve the watch and want to check in with Arden.

I clear my throat, key the mic, and try to raise Arden on Channel 68. "Tug *Alanna Rose* to the *Arden McHale*." Little Hal is at the wheel, cracking a smile as he pretends to ignore me.

I'm about to switch back to Channel 13 when I hear Arden respond. "John? John? How'd you know I'd be home on a workday?"

"Lucky guess," I say. There's a patch of silence, and my stomach tightens when I realize Arden may not be alone. There are plenty of reasons people stay home from work. I don't want Chase to be hers.

"I was totally out of it when I woke up," she says. "For a girl who likes to think she doesn't need much sleep to function, I really slammed into a wall at warp speed."

"I know what you mean. And luckily, I didn't hit any walls."

Her laughter fills the wheelhouse. "So I'm laying low today, resting up," she says. "And a song from the wheelhouse sure would go a long way."

"I guess I've got a few minutes before I'm on watch. And as long as Little Hal doesn't mind." I wrap a rubber band around the mic twice before hanging it off the handle of the starboard side spotlight.

There is something about playing for Arden that completely fucks with my equilibrium. I'm used to performing for a nonexistent audience, not a woman sitting in her apartment and actually listening. I decide to play "Hitch My Soul," a song I'd written years ago when I was wondering what it would be like to meet the person I'd fall in love with.

"Tug *Alanna Rose* to the *Arden McHale*," I say. "I'm closer than you think."

Chapter Nineteen: Arden

Thursday, May 19, 1994

I stare at the radio as John starts to sing. The fact I've only been with him for a handful of minutes doesn't dilute how tangible he appears to me. The image I see holds the depth of his gaze and smoothness of his movement. I imagine quietly walking up behind him to place my hands on his shoulders while he plays, breathing him in.

I stretch out on the couch to take in the rest of the serenade when my phone rings. I decide to let the machine pick up, but then the ringing stops and starts again.

Afraid it might be Macy or Marva with news about Levi, I drag myself into kitchen to pick it up. "Hello."

"Arden?" It's Chase. Again. "You sound annoyed. Am I interrupting something?"

"I'm just in the middle . . ." I start to say without finishing my thought.

"Why don't you just call me back when you're free?" he asks, sounding annoyed too.

"What's up, Chase?" I don't want to call him back.

"How's meeting at six tonight?" I don't respond right away, listening for John's singing in the gap between Chase's question and my pending answer. "Arden? Are you even paying attention?"

"Lighten up," I snap.

I hear John's voice—not singing now, but calling my name. "Just give me a minute, Chase. I'll be right back." I place the cradle down on the counter and run over to the radio, pressing the mic. "John?"

"Did I put you to sleep?"

"No, no. I'm on the couch, lost in thought. I don't know what to say. Your music is . . . thank you."

"I'm about to be on watch here," he says. "Garrett's down in the galley. All's well. Is there a good time to call and talk to Marva and Macy?"

"We're all having dinner tonight. Will you be in the harbor for a while?" I look out the window at the river alive with movement and color, reveling in the thought of John being nearby.

"Yeah. We're heading to Boston tomorrow morning. How about you radio me when everyone gets to your place? Around six thirty?"

"Sounds good. I'll talk to you then. And thanks, really, for the songs. You made my day."

"You must not be having much of a day then. Try to make it a better one, would you?"

"I'll give it my best shot. 'Bye. I mean. I mean over. I mean over and out. I mean . . . What the hell do I say here?"

"Talk to you later's fine."

I pick up the phone again, wondering if Chase's sour mood is here to stay. "Hey," I say. "Sorry about that. It was John checking in to see when he could call for Garrett to talk to Marva and Macy."

"You were just talking to John?" he asks.

"I was indeed. Does six thirty work? Then we can all go out to eat or just order in. It would probably be more comfortable to stay here."

Chase's mood softens a bit. "Not a bad idea," he says. "We'll be there at six thirty. And about last night . . ." He pauses, and I wonder if he's waiting for me to stop him midsentence and brush the whole thing off. When I don't say anything, he continues, speaking slowly. "I thought there was something between us. I felt it that night we walked from the gallery to the restaurant. I saw it in your eyes at Mulvaney's. Am I wrong?"

He's right. I had been attracted to him. I liked being around him. And that morning when I was so broken up about Billy, Chase was exactly what I needed him to be—spontaneous, a good listener, funny, *there*.

"How did you get to be so . . . direct?" I ask. "I could use a few lessons."

"I've got good motivation. I care about you. I thought we were heading in some sort of direction—toward each other, I guess. And then it's like a wall went up."

"I can't always explain how I'm feeling or why. But I can tell you that you're right that things shifted between us. I thought we were getting closer too . . ."

"And then . . ." he prompts.

"Does there always have to be a why?" I ask, not backing down.

"Yeah, for me there does, because there always is," he says. "It's whether or not you have the courage to be honest."

"I'm starting to feel like this is an inquisition. Can you please take it down a notch?"

"Can I?" he asks. "Yes. Will I? That's another question entirely." He forces a laugh.

"Will you?" I ask, playing along.

"I will," he says. "I'll back all the way down and just step out of your life if that's easier for you now. Whether or not you want to admit it, you do know why things cooled off between us. At least I believe you do."

"You're not going to drop this, are you?"

"It's John, isn't it, Arden? Something clicked between the two of you."

"Whoa, you're way ahead of me. There's nothing I can say about John right now."

"And then there's what you won't say."

I am getting angry. "You know what, Chase? You've got a lot of nerve. I just lost my best friend, and you seem to forget it's *my* family that's in trouble."

"Give me a break. You're something else, Arden."

"I'm something else, all right. Tell you what, I think it's a good idea if you bow out completely right now. We don't need you to help us deal with Levi."

"I'll be at your apartment at six thirty tonight," he says. "You can be the one to explain to Marva and Macy why you don't want me there." Click.

I keep my fingers wrapped tightly around the phone as adrenalin rushes through me. Is my life just going to keep crumbling into little bits strewn all over the city while I wander around like a wayward Gretel trying to find my way back to the way it used to be?

I open a couple of windows and turn on some music. My apartment feels stale, and my body needs to be in motion. First, I strip the bed. Then I pick up the clothes heaped on the floor. I get the washing machine going, feeling energized by its steady chug and the mundane task of restoring order to my court.

I clean the bathroom, dust the living room, vacuum, and sweep. I scrub the kitchen sink, run the dishwasher, and clear any and all science experiments out of the fridge. By the time I finish making my bed, it's almost six and time for a shower.

When the steady stream of hot water hits my back, I finally allow myself to think about Chase. He is right about us. And he is right about John, even if I have no way of knowing what is next. Is John still wondering about us too?

I'm grateful for the hot shower and the invigorating smell of rosemary ginseng soap. It's good to step out of my bathroom into a freshly scrubbed apartment, and I feel much more prepared for the night ahead.

Chapter Twenty: John

Thursday, May 20, 1993

Garrett beams as he reaches up to deliver a wallop of a high five, totally amped up to talk to his mom and Grandma Macy. I don't get the sense that he's homesick so much as looking forward to sharing his adventures on the high seas and telling them all about his new best friend, Little Hal.

And me? After almost twenty years on tugs, I know a thing or two about how the brain operates when left to its own devices, even though I chose to ignore that hard-earned knowledge when I'd decided singing for Arden was a good idea.

I'm more than a little annoyed with myself. Yes, I'm attracted to Arden, but I'm also no stranger to the magnetic power of circumstance. Both losing Billy and helping her family has shifted us into overdrive. Will I feel the same attraction in a few weeks when things have settled down? The only research I have to drawn on is from my lifelong inability to stay connected to anyone. So should I even consider getting involved with Arden? Absolutely not.

I also know that when it comes to Chase, I shouldn't underestimate my competitive nature. Sometimes I don't even care what I am competing for, as long as I win. I smile at the memory of how Billy used to ride me about my intensity. "You come off as this chill guy, but deep down you're a cauldron of competitive whoop-ass. When you want what you want, you go balls to the *wall* until you get it." I think about how relieved I was when

Chase and Arden showed up at Macy's building separately yesterday. I'd almost willed them *not* to get out of a shared cab. Was that born of my feelings for Arden or more about not wanting Chase in the game?

Now it's almost time for the family radio rendezvous. I plan to call on the early side, hoping to reach Arden while she's still alone, but I can tell Garrett has more on his mind than talking to his family. "Can I ask you something?" His face is solemn.

"Anything," I reply, equally serious.

"Why are Little Hal and Benny the only ones who like me? I mean, the other guys, they'll say, 'Hey, kid,' or nod at me, but no one else tries to talk to me. It's like I'm not even here."

I don't share how I told the crew to do just that . . . pretend Garrett wasn't even aboard so I didn't have to worry about all the possible combustive situations, not to mention the plentiful stream of colorful language that could scar even the toughest eight-year-old.

"That's the thing about the guys on a tugboat crew. They're used to keeping to themselves. They're loners."

"They talk to each other, though," he says. "That is, until I'm around, and then they clam right up."

I'm surprised—and impressed—by how seriously they've taken my avoidance order. "Listen, Little Hal is the coolest guy on this boat. And Benny? What can I say? If you've got them talking to you, that's all that matters."

"Arden McHale to Tug *Alanna Rose*. Do you read me?" It's Arden's voice, joining us in the wheelhouse.

"Tug *Alanna Rose* to the *Arden McHale*," I respond. "Garrett's here with me. Gang arrived yet?"

"No, not yet. But Chase is pretty punctual. I expect them to be here any minute."

"Chase seems like a punctual guy," I say. "Very buttoned up." Silence. Has the sarcasm in my voice annoyed her? "Arden?"

"I'm still here. Is Garrett with you?"

"He sure is."

"Um . . . some things have changed since you left yesterday." Before I can respond, she clicks back in with, "They're here. Let me open the door." It's true that some radio silence is louder than others. What the hell is going on?

"Garrett," I say, waving him down from his stool perch.

He barrels over, grabbing the mic. I've shown him how it works and smile at his apparent confidence. "Mom? Grandma Macy?" He lets go and waits, peering up at me. I nod and smile. The kid really listens, and he's proven himself to be a master of keeping himself occupied.

"Garrett, honey, it's me, Grandma Macy. We miss you!"

"And I'm here," another voice says. "I mean, it's me, Mom. It's Mom. You sound so close."

"I *am* close," Garrett says. "We're floating on the East River, right outside."

"What have you been up to?" Marva asks.

"Well, everybody likes my cooking. And I've learned a lot about stars and sea chanteys and how to draw a boat so it looks like it's getting smaller as it moves toward the horizon."

"Wow, all that in just a day?" Macy asks. "You've been busy."

Garrett squirms, his body a barometer of how hard it is for him to keep a lid on his excitement. "Captain John is the best. And Little Hal too. He hasn't let his bad luck with women make him a bitter man."

I laugh as Marva says, "Well, that's good to hear. I'm sure he likes having you around."

"We're heading up to Boston soon. And maybe Maine from there, so I won't be able to talk to you for a few days. Maybe even the rest of the trip," Garrett reports. I'm glad his voice sounds upbeat.

"Oh, is that so?" Macy says. "We'll miss you, but it's so good to hear you're having fun.

"So much fun!" Garrett practically shouts.

"I love you," Marva says. "We all love you. And we can't wait to hear from you again and to see you and give you some hugs."

"Dad been around?" Garrett asks, his expression unchanged.

"No, he hasn't," Marva answers, "and don't you go worrying about your dad."

"Has he called?" The kid isn't giving up.

"Did you hear what your mother just told you to do? Don't worry," Macy says. "Focus on where you are and what you're doing. Don't worry about your mom and me—and *don't* worry about your daddy."

"Is Chase there?" Garrett asks. I can picture Chase's face lighting up at being remembered.

"I'm here," Chase says.

"I'm a chief mate, Chase. I really help out. Little Hal says I'll be king of the wheelhouse in no time."

"No doubt," Chase says.

"Can I talk to Arden?" Garrett asks.

"Sure can. Hold on." There's a quick pause and then Arden's voice. "Hey, Garrett. Sounds like you're a born sailor."

"You're lucky to have a friend like Captain John," he says. "He's really something."

I wonder if Arden's face is burning hot like mine. "You've got that right," she says. "He's a great guy."

"I'm gonna go down to the galley and rassle up some dessert," Garrett says. "Hopefully Darryl didn't eat all the ice cream sandwiches."

"Love you," Marva says. "Keep on being good and listening to Captain John."

"Aye, aye, Mom." Garrett hands me the mic with a wave.

"I feel much better now knowing everything is working out," Marva says. "Thank you."

"You really don't have to thank me, He's a great kid. And he's out of earshot now. Any word from Levi?"

"We don't know where he is," Marva says. "He hasn't called lately, but he should be in the city by now."

"I know you'll figure things out tonight," I say, wondering if I should just radio the police anonymously. Maybe Chase already has? The longer they stay under the radar, the more power they're giving Levi. Hopefully,

Arden and Chase will be able to talk some sense into them tonight. "Garrett's right about our schedule," I continue. "We're going to Boston tomorrow and then maybe Maine. There won't be another check-in until we get to a port, and then he'll call you from a phone."

"Oh, on the phone, right," Marva says. "We won't be at the apartment, so call Arden, OK?"

"Is she nearby?" I ask, knowing she must be.

"She's right here," Marva answers.

"You rang?" Arden asks.

"I'll check in with you tomorrow before we head north," I say. "And I'm going to be on later. Probably around eleven thirty."

I hope she gets that I'm talking about the Wheelhouse Café, but I'm not sure she understands, because she says, "Sounds like you've got a busy night ahead. Good luck. And good night, John. Thanks again."

"Good night." The silence that follows is big. And deep. I'm tired of being thanked. All I want is to be in the apartment with them, and I feel a million miles away.

Before my thoughts have a chance to spiral, I start jotting down a set list. Three songs. Maybe four. I choose each one for Arden, hoping she'll get to hear it.

Chapter Twenty-One: Arden

Thursday, May 19, 1994

I miss John the moment his voice leaves the room. I'm grateful to have company; even though it means talking about Levi and dealing with Chase's tense energy, I need something to focus on.

I had ordered pizza and put a stack of paper plates and napkins on the coffee table. Chase doesn't waste any time getting the conversation started. "Arden and I have given this a lot of thought, and we agree the authorities have to be part of the game plan. A big part."

The authorities sounds so 1970s bad-cop TV show. "We reported Levi once," Marva says. "It was a fiasco, and he was furious."

"We need to do more than just report him," Chase says. "We need to document the history of his abuse. The effect he's had on your family."

"Don't you know how these stories end? When all is said and done, it's still us against Levi," Macy says. "What are they going to do, station a cop outside our door and assign bodyguards to follow us around? Don't think so."

"I'm not saying that a police report is the whole solution, but it's got to be part of it," Chase said. "And I'll do it with you—get it on paper, go down to the station, whatever it takes. The restraining order you have may have expired. Do you know?"

Marva keeps her gaze low as she shakes her head. "What else can we do? There's got to be something else."

I know how much hope they must have had coming to this meeting. Chase is a problem solver. They probably expected him to show up with a long list of ways to make Levi go away.

I inch toward the edge of the couch as if something is pushing me to speak, hoping that if I have the courage to start talking, I'll stop feeling like a little girl. "I've never told either of you about this before, but I lost one of my best friends—Casey Flynn, do remember her?—because her mom didn't want the police involved. Mrs. Flynn said she didn't need the whole town watching their family unravel." I realize it sounds like Casey died, which is what it felt like when she disappeared. "She's not dead. At least, I don't think she is. I haven't seen her since our senior year of high school. One night, Casey went home determined to convince her mom that moving out was no longer an option. It was the only thing that would keep her alive."

I exhale. Casey's bravery had been fueled by Jack Daniels mixed with festering anger. That combination hadn't helped when she found her dad pressing her mom's hands onto the front burner of the stove, threatening to turn it on *again* if she didn't shut the fuck up. Casey had grabbed a sledgehammer from the side porch and rushed back in to smack him across the back. Then she left.

"What happened?" Marva asks, reaching for my hand.

"The night was a disaster. Casey disappeared. And then her parents ended up staying together until her dad died in a car accident about a year later. Now her mom only leaves the house after midnight to stock up on whatever she can find at the gas station store down the block."

"I'm so sorry to hear about Casey," Chase says. "I didn't know." He looks at me softly. "You could semidisappear," Chase suggests, shifting the conversation and his gaze over to Marva and Macy.

"I'm not gonna let that asshole turn our lives upside down," Marva says, tears flashing in her eyes.

"Your life is already turned upside down," Chase says. "And he already hurt you. I can't stand to think of him doing that again. Or of Garrett watching something happen to you. You're his rock."

"What do you mean, 'semidisappear'?" I ask.

"Well, nothing as drastic as the Witness Protection Program, but a new address, for starters."

"And whether or not you move, Garrett's school needs to know what's going on," I say. "It's the only way they can help you keep him safe."

"That's where the authorities come in," Chase continues. "And as you're friend, I'd be irresponsible if I didn't keep repeating how crucial it is that you stop keeping Levi a secret."

"I don't want Garrett treated any differently in school," Marva says. "He's such a good boy."

"The school cares about Garrett. You have to trust in that," I say.

"They care about him, sure," Macy says, "but they've got their hands full. Can they really keep a close eye on one little boy?"

Chase is adamant, "First, we alert the authorities—the police and Garrett's school. Then you move to a new apartment and get an unlisted phone number."

"What about my jobs?" Marva asks.

"You said Levi doesn't know about either one, right?" I ask. She nods. "That's good."

The room settles into silence. Aunt Macy slides closer to Marva and reaches over to squeeze her hand. "We keep wishing for a way out of this, and I know neither one of us wants to believe that there's really only one option. We know what we need to do. We need to listen to Chase and Arden and just get it all out there."

"He'll find us. He'll always find us," Marva whispers, breaking Macy's gaze to stare at her lap.

"You give him too much credit," Macy says. "He can't get out of his own way. We've just been making it too easy for him."

"I'm so tired," Marva says. "From the inside out. I just want Levi to go away."

"Well, since he's not going to disappear, we have to," Macy says. "I cannot—*will not*—bear the thought of him hurting you again. Watching him slam you against the wall and then cut off your beautiful, beautiful hair was one of the . . ."

Marva reaches over to clutch onto Aunt Macy. "Shh, Mama. I'm OK. Let's not talk about what's done. It's done."

Macy breaks away to grab Marva by both shoulders. "It's not done yet, but I am. I'm done being afraid and ashamed. Thinking about that night makes me so angry. How did we give Levi so much control over us? I'm done with him, Marva. *Done.* I'm a powerful woman, and I'm not gonna let that hopped-up jackass make us feel like we're trapped any longer. No more." She turns to Chase. "You've done so much for us, and I hate to ask you for anything else, but would you really come with us tomorrow? To the police?" Marva nods in agreement, slowly at first and then quickly, as she leans her head on Macy's shoulder.

Chase and I have both been sitting statue-like on the outskirts of their discussion. He slides to the edge of the couch and puts out his arms so each woman can grab a hand. "I'm here for you. Of course I'll go with you."

Marva starts sobbing, and I go into the bathroom to grab a box of tissues. I hear Aunt Macy's voice. "You didn't expect all this when you signed up for tango lessons, did you? I feel like all we've ever done is burden you, and I can't wait till the day we can have you over for dinner and just talk about the weather."

Chase is smiling as I hand Marva the tissues. "This is the beginning of the end of all this," he says. "How about I get you home, and we figure out our game plan for tomorrow?"

As Marva and Aunt Macy surround me with a flurry of good-byes, Chase walks into the hallway without acknowledging me. I avoid looking at him, too, not wanting our eyes to meet.

Then my door clicks shut, and I'm left alone with an uneasy feeling. Why am I having a hard time believing everything is going all right?

I pick up the phone, slamming down the receiver when I realize I'm about to dial Billy's number. I close my eyes and issue an order: "Go to sleep, Arden. Just go to sleep."

Chapter Twenty-Two: John

Thursday, May 19, 1994

Garrett is tucked into his rack. I imagine him flipping through a book by the glow of the overhead lamp. Little Hal is still at the helm, sipping lukewarm green tea from a giant mug. The wheelhouse is quiet.

I pick up the mic and turn the radio dial to Channel 68. Before I invite anyone else into the café, I want to make sure Arden is going to be in the audience. "Tug *Alanna Rose* to the *Arden McHale*."

"Finally," her voice responds. "This night has been on the slow boat to eleven thirty."

"I wasn't sure if you caught my hint."

"Are you kidding? You *know* I hang on your every word, Captain John." Her voice is playful, and it brings my entire body to attention.

"In that case, how about a song?" I ask.

"That's what I'm here for."

"No falling asleep this time. And if your phone rings . . ."

"I'll ignore it," she says, "but I do want to give you some good news before you start. Marva and Macy are going to the police with Chase tomorrow to file a report. And I think they're going to move too."

"Wow," I say. "That's big."

"It was pretty intense, the whole conversation tonight," she says. I've just been sitting here thinking about everything since Chase left to bring them home."

"Well, now you can just sit there and listen," I say.

"Hold on," she says. "Someone's at the door."

I have a feeling I know who it is and wish I'd tacked not answering the door onto my no-phone-call rule. A few drawn-out moments of silence preceded Arden's return to the mic with, "John, Chase is here. He brought Marva and Macy home to pick up some things so they could stay at a friend's apartment. He walked them all the way inside, but it didn't matter because he was waiting, crouched in the maintenance closet or hiding in the shadows somewhere."

I had to stop her. "Arden," I say. "Slow down. *Who* was waiting?"

"Levi. He was there. In the building. Waiting for them. They were in their apartment packing a bag. *Safe.* Marva walked downstairs first to meet Chase in the lobby. That's when Levi jumped out from behind a duct and grabbed her. He grabbed her, John. And he was trying to drag her back into the apartment when Aunt Macy came out and pushed him. She pushed him so hard he fell over Marva and tumbled down the first flight of stairs. Aunt Macy said he looked more like a pile of laundry dumped on the landing than a person. They thought he was dead." Arden's sobs are punctuated with short, sharp breaths.

"Arden, hey, slow down. It's OK. Everything's OK."

"I know it is," she says. "Now more than ever, right? Levi's pretty busted up, but he's alive. And the police found a gun and a few bags of heroin on him, so he's not going anywhere when he leaves the hospital. He had a gun, John. Can you imagine if Garrett had been home? I'm so glad he's with you."

I'm relieved, but I also feel trapped. Chase is where I want to be—next to Arden. There's nothing I can do except say it aloud so she'd know. "Arden, I wish I was there with you right now."

"I don't know why I'm having such a hard time with this," Arden says. "I mean, it's all good, right? Levi's out of the picture. Marva and Macy are safe. Garrett is safe. But I'm still feeling churned up. I should probably just crawl into bed."

Alone. I think. Just add the word *alone.* She doesn't, but she does keep talking. "Any time my emotions surge, I land back at Billy. I get all mixed up and can't think about anything else except how much I miss him, and how sorry I am that . . ." She stops midsentence. "Never mind. I should go. I need to get a grip."

I'm not ready to let her go. "Should I bring Garrett back?" I ask. "I mean, before I head up to Boston."

"Oh, I hadn't thought about that."

"Otherwise, it's possible I won't be back in New York again for a week, maybe two, depending on where we go from Boston."

"I can't believe you've only been gone since yesterday. It seems like forever." She pauses. "Garrett should come home. That would be best." Another pause. "Chase agrees. Where and when?"

Chase agrees. "I'll meet you at the Battery tomorrow morning at five thirty. I'll nose the tug up to the wall to let Garrett off. We shouldn't draw too much attention at that hour."

"OK," Arden says. "We'll be there. And thanks, John. Really. For everything."

I don't know if she hears me say, "See you soon," but I am sure soon won't be soon enough for me. The pounding in my chest taunts me, each beat reminding me that salt air and distance aren't going to change the way I feel about Arden.

Chapter Twenty-Three: Arden

Wednesday, June 1, 1994

As I wait for John to get back, the stretch of days feels like summertime when I was a kid. Each day back then had seemed to mirror me—elastic and inexhaustible. I try to conjure up that childlike ease of being wrapped in the now, but it's impossible for me to trick myself into focusing on anything other than how each day seems to show off its ability to disperse every second with a slow, methodical tick. The only distraction that works is work itself. The trash basket by my office door is overflowing with takeout containers and coffee cups, a testament to just how distracted I have needed to be.

Now, less than forty-eight hours after we watched the *Alanna Rose* pull out of Erie Basin, Chase and I are standing at the Battery in the shadow of the Twin Towers, awaiting her return. We exchange a handful of words. There isn't much left to say, and I wonder if he shares my awareness that this might be the last time we're around each other alone.

The morning sky glows a quiet pink that rapidly crescendos into something much louder as it heralds in a parade of wispy clouds. We can see a long red dash getting larger as it moves slowly toward us, and we hear the engines of the *Alanna Rose* purring with a barely audible, hypnotic whir. I keep my gaze on the red wheelhouse. It looks like a solid cylinder at first, and then the windows catch some of the morning light and wink at me.

Chase stands a few feet away from me. Even though he may be vibrating with sadness and confusion, I know he's going to see this through and make sure Garrett is safe. Chase is the kind of guy who eats his carrots because his mother once told him to, and he still doesn't want to let her down.

The night before, he tried to comfort me as I sobbed. I'm not used to crying by myself, let alone in front of anyone else. Something about the relief of Marva and Macy—and ultimately Garrett—being safe had triggered uncontrollable tears.

My body had stayed tense and distant as Chase held me. I hadn't even let my head drop down to his chest. "Jesus, Arden," he'd said, letting go of me to take a step back. "What's with you? I'm just trying to be a friend. Can't I even comfort you?"

I remained rigid as I slowly raised my head to look him in the eye. "I need to be alone, Chase. I'm sorry. I don't even have the head space to make sense of it all for myself, let alone explain it to you or anyone else."

"I know you're acting like this is because of John . . ."

"Would you just stop it? *I lost my best friend, Chase.* I haven't even had time to understand what that means, and you won't stop pushing me. You pretend to be here for me, but you're really here for you, aren't you?"

I had told myself that the look on Chase's face was one of someone whose true motives had been revealed, but it was probably more like hurt and surprise.

"I know you're used to getting what you want, and you can't have me. It's driving you insane." I spoke these sentences slowly. There was an echo in my head and a gnawing ache below my rib cage, that thick, heavy feeling I get when I feel like a human avalanche, someone who wants to stop rolling but keeps getting more and more out of control.

"You don't have to say another word. I thought you were someone else, but you used me. It's that simple. I get it. I get you." Chase had stormed out, slamming the door so hard the room vibrated. I was grateful for the punctuation of inanimate objects. There was nothing left to say.

There *was* something left to do, though, and that was to meet the *Alanna Rose* at five thirty in the morning. After drifting in and out of sleep, I woke to a dark room and peered out at the shard of charcoal sky. Part of me had that "waking up early for a trip" feeling from my childhood, when it didn't matter what I put on or if I felt like talking, because I'd soon be asleep in the back seat as we headed for an amusement park or Aunt Georgia's or the airport.

Chase got to the Battery first, of course. "Good morning," I say.

"Hi," he answers, staring out at the harbor with his hands shoved in his pockets. We are a pathetic pair. He looks worn out and adrift. My eyes are puffy from sobbing into my pillow. Neither one of us attempts to clear the air with apologies or small talk, so Garrett's voice is the first one we hear after our halfhearted hellos. "Land ho!" he bellows from the bow.

Chase cups his hands around his mouth to shout, "Garrett, looking good, buddy!"

Garrett jumps and waves. He also appears to be shouting something else, but I can't hear him anymore. I listen to the engines pull back with a grinding rumble as the boat decelerates, and then I follow Chase as he walks out to the spot the bow pointed toward. I still haven't seen John.

There are certain memories I carry around like sensory snapshots—the moldy, liverwurst-infused smell of carpet that nearly knocked me out as I searched under a stranger's couch for a bracelet I wasn't supposed to borrow from my sister, and the dizzying pattern on a cloth napkin—Mallard ducks and cattails—I'd stared at as the first guy who made me blush showered me with compliments. And how could I forget the milestones? You know, the earthy, cactus-cum-velvet texture of tequila fumes that seemed to carry my triumphant feet onto the risers at high school graduation or the collective clank of halyards kissing their masts the morning my dad sailed *Andromeda* to our dock and said, "She's yours."

John appearing behind Garrett—seemingly out of nowhere—is a snapshot I know will forever define how I remember the month of June. John embodies it fully—a promise of warmth and expectation and everything meaningful that has been patiently waiting, dormant under an unforgiving winter landscape, until it couldn't be contained any longer. The moment deserves a musical score—something triumphant and bold, with a few well-placed cymbal crashes.

That's when the here and now of the situation kicks in. Commands are shouted. Bags are tossed. The tugboat's bow gently yet boldly presses up against the wall. John passes Garrett down into Chase's open arms. Chase and John exchange nods. John and I have a few seconds to soak each other in. I am sure our thoughts are in sync—issued and accepted invitations to see what's next. John's steady gaze offers me the option to be the first one to turn away, and I take it, knowing it will be easier for me to walk over to Chase and Garrett than to watch the *Alanna Rose* retreat back into the harbor.

Chase obviously has no intention of hanging around. He's already stowed Garrett's bags in the trunk of an idling cab, even though we hadn't spoken about who would bring him home. "We're heading out," he says without looking at me. "Somehow I figured you'd be staying longer and told Marva I'd get Garrett home . . ." Garrett interrupts Chase, running over to hug me. "'Bye, Arden. You'll come over soon, right?"

"Of course. I need to hear about what it's like to be a chief mate."

"It'll have to be later, Arden. We're going to have breakfast with Grandma Macy now," he says. "I'll bet she's making something special."

I keep my focus on Garrett as he slides into the back seat. Chase clicks the door shut behind him before opening his own. He starts the car and drives away. No window rolled down. No sideways glance or lackluster wave. Not even an enthusiastic middle finger. I stand there long after they drive away.

* * *

That's when the waiting begins. Any time in my apartment is time spent circling the radio. I know John's somewhere between New York and Boston, but once in a while I still flip through the channels just to hear the harbor come to life and marvel that this alternate universe right outside my window has existed undetected for so long.

I think of all the times Billy had been right there in the harbor, maybe even looking over to find my slice of Manhattan, wondering what I was doing, who I was with. I consider going to Greenport to visit his parents but find it impossible to drag myself away from hiding out in my daily routine. Even the two hours spent driving east on the Long Island Expressway would give me too much time to think.

John leaves two messages in thirteen days. Both times I slam my fist on the table next to the answering machine, cursing the fact I hadn't been home to pick up the phone. The first message is long and rambling, with lots of details about his day. The second message is shorter, and there's lots of background noise—voices and clanging. He tells me he's supposed to be back Friday the ninth for a shift change, and I laugh that he thinks I need a reminder. I feel like I've been lugging around an oversized calendar and a giant red magic marker, crossing off each day.

Then yesterday I hear, "Tug *Alanna Rose* to the *Arden McHale*." I'm on the couch eating vegetable lo mein out of the carton and catapult myself toward the radio to grab the mic. The noodles topple over onto the coffee table, and the chopsticks land on the floor.

"It's me, John," I say quickly. "I mean, John, it's me, Arden."

"I get off the boat tomorrow. Can you meet me?"

"What time? Where?"

"About three. Erie Basin."

"3 p.m.?" I ask, hoping I'm wrong so I have fewer hours to count between now and then.

"You've got it. I'll be there."

"I'll be there," I echo.

The next morning, I go to the office giddy with anticipation. Everything seems snappier, brighter—whether I'm refilling a stapler or calling a client to talk about a brochure. The day flows purposefully toward three o'clock.

I imagine our reunion rolling out a dozen different ways. Each scenario begins the same, though, with me standing on the dock as the *Alanna Rose* pulls in. I leave the office right after lunch to make sure I have plenty of time to get to Erie Basin.

* * *

I shouldn't have been concerned about missing John's arrival. I catch sight of the *Alanna Rose* at about two thirty and then have to wait for her to get to the dock. A few men are standing near me, and only one of them acknowledges my presence with a clipped, "Hello." The others seem absorbed with smoking, talking in muffled voices, and staring at the *Alanna Rose*. When the boat ties up, they hop right on and join in the activity on deck.

What can you say about a moment that you've scribbled in pencil, erased, and drawn again for days? For all my yearning, I have to fight the urge to turn and run away. Even though I remind myself not to let expectations take root, they're blooming with wild abandon. I think the only thing keeping me still is my inability to move my legs. They seem to be fastened to the dock.

So I'm standing motionless when John jumps down from the *Alanna Rose*. There's no running to meet each other. I feel paralyzed, and it's starting to border on comical. John drops his bag, placing his guitar case at my feet to open his arms wide. I fall into him then and revel in how someone so new to me can feel so much like home.

"Can I interest you in a field trip to Greenport?" he asks, kissing the top of my head and leaving his lips there.

"Now?"

"Right now. I just feel like being there. With you."

Spontaneity is not my middle name. In fact, *spontaneous* wouldn't show up on a list of a hundred adjectives that describe me. I am a girl who likes a plan.

"How are we going to get there?" I'm stalling for time while I try to imagine being able to just leave.

"My truck," he says, pointing to the lone blue pickup in the lot. "You sound like you need some convincing, am I right?"

"Not exactly. You just happened to touch on one of my character flaws within three minutes of being home."

"And that would be?"

"An inability to drop everything and just *go*. I need a plan to be spontaneous, if that makes any sense."

"I wouldn't call that a character flaw. And the invitation stands, so do you want to go to Greenport with me right now?"

I allow myself to look at him. *Really* look at him. How is it possible for John to be so completely present? I can feel him right here, in this moment, not thinking about Garrett and Chase or docking the tug or even getting in the truck with me and starting the ignition. I want to be in that space with him. Hell, who am I kidding? I want to be alone with him. Anywhere.

"I'm in," I say. "Let's go."

I pick up his bag, grab his hand, and pull him toward his truck, letting the energy of the moment run through me. John manages to scoop up his guitar without letting go of my grip and runs up beside me. When we get to the truck, he places his guitar in the bed and takes the bag from my hands to toss that in too. Then he looks at me sternly as I try to open the door. "What do you think you're doing, Arden?"

"Oh, is it locked?" I ask as he puts his hands on either side of my waist and turns me to lean against the door. He presses against me and gives me one soft kiss and then another, pulling gently on my bottom lip.

"No," he says. "It's not worth locking, but you're crazy if you think I'm letting you open your own door. You're with a Greenport boy now, Miss McHale. Get used to being treated like a lady."

I put one hand behind his neck and the other around his waist, pulling him in for another kiss, and this one goes from leisurely to urgent.

"I think we've got a long ride ahead of us," I say when I accomplish the nearly impossible task of removing my lips from his.

"You can say that again," he says, moving in again. We both laugh midkiss, and then he reaches behind me to open the door. "And the Long Island Expressway is only the beginning."

"Are you going to entertain me with your repertoire of sea chanteys?" I ask when he slides into the driver's seat. "I'm all ears." I rest my head on the seat and close my eyes, smiling.

John starts the truck, and I hear his seat belt click as he gives me a kiss on the cheek. "I'm hoping you'll sing for me this time around," he says. "*I'm all ears.*"

"Sure. Let me flip through my jukebox." I pretend to press a button and react to each invisible song. "No, don't know you well enough to sing *that* song. Hmm . . . that one will put you to sleep, and I can't be responsible for you dozing at the wheel." I pause. "By John, I think I've got it! This is a song Billy and I used to perform on karaoke night at Whiskey Wind. He told me he had a Brandy in every port on the Eastern Seaboard. Feel free to join in if the spirit moves you."

"Or if you sound so awful you leave me with no choice?" he asks, playfully squeezing my thigh.

I giggle and can't remember the last time I'd been caught up in being silly. It is intoxicating. Maybe that's why I actually have the courage to sing, "There's a port on a western bay, and it serves a hundred ships a day; Lonely sailors pass the time away and talk about their homes."

"Not bad, not bad at all," John says loudly as my voice rises into the second verse. "And Looking Glass would be very impressed that someone actually knows the words to something other than the chorus."

He joins me then, and our voices come together to belt out, "And the sailors say, 'Brandy, you're a fine girl. What a good wife you would be. Yeah, your eyes could steal a sailor from the sea. Do do-do do-do-do, Do do-do- do-do-do . . .'"

We barrel through the song, rolling the windows down so the wind vibrates through the cab, whipping my hair around. When we sing, "But my life, my lover, my lady is the sea," I think about how being aware of tugboat syndrome hadn't made me immune to it. I'm allowing myself to get wrapped up in John, still believing that the sea and how it takes hold of people I care about will just be a backdrop for all that is to come, not a central character.

Chapter Twenty-Four: John

Wednesday, June 1, 1994

I usually expect the LIE to defend its "longest parking lot in the world" title, but Arden and I seem to be on a supersonic conveyor belt. We make it to Riverhead in about an hour, and it'll only be another thirty minutes until we pull into Greenport—unless we get stuck behind a farm tractor.

I share a few stories about Garrett in rare form on the *Alanna Rose*, and she fills me in on everything that has happened with his family. Then we ride in silence for a while, and I think Arden's nodded off until she says, "I wonder if Chase is going to stay involved with Garrett. I know what happened between Chase and me doesn't have to affect their relationship, but it's weird to think of him being involved in my family's life but completely disconnected from mine."

"What happened, Arden?" I wonder if I want to know.

"It's more what didn't happen. When I didn't respond to Chase the way he wanted me to, he kept on trying to figure out why." She shakes her head and rolls her window up halfway. "He was right about some things. That's what made the situation really suck in the end." She sighs, and it's almost like she's talking to herself. "I did like being around Chase, and yeah, I was attracted to him. Not just the way he looks, but the way he swims through life unaffected by rough seas and riptides. And he was really there for me when I got back from Billy's funeral. That first day was surreal and . . ." I'm part curious, part nauseous, and part relieved as she continues. "But I'd met you, and even though I wasn't conscious of what was happening, Chase picked up on it and was almost belligerent in his efforts to make me admit I had feelings for you."

After getting by with nods and one or two word exchanges on the boat, I sometimes struggle to say what's on my mind. "Arden," I begin, "there's no doubt that Chase is a good guy, and he's absolutely crazy about you. That's evident. I actually worried I'd come home to find the two of you closer than ever."

"Wow, that can't be easy for you to admit. I don't take you as someone who's used to worrying about not getting the girl."

"If I seem that self-assured, maybe I should think about acting? Set my sights on an Oscar?"

"But you're not acting," she says. "It's just who you are. You have this innate confidence that makes people relax."

We're on the North Fork and getting close to Greenport now, reminiscing about the drive-in movie theater that used to be on the outskirts of the village next to the Lutheran Church. "All this talk about the drive-in is making me think about you and me in a back seat," I say.

"Last time I checked, you didn't have a back seat."

"I can still have fun imagining us stretched out in one. And to your point, not only are we without a back seat, we don't even really have a place we can be alone together, do we?"

"You're right, and don't blame me, Mr. Spontaneous. This field trip was *your* brilliant idea."

"Maybe it's not a bad thing. Hell, who knows? We could be halfway to a heartache if I hadn't left on the tug. And what if we weren't faced with the logistical challenges of not having our own place to sleep in Greenport tonight?"

"What then?"

"We'd be in bed right now, that's what. And we'd probably never leave."

"Mm," she answers. "Those scenarios sound just awful. Thank God for tugboats and logistical challenges."

"And lucky for you, resourceful is my middle name," I say with a smirk. We pass the high school and I ask, "OK if we stop by my Aunt Suebee's?"

"Sure. No one's expecting me. I don't have anyplace to be." She claps her hands together and shrugs her shoulders, relishing what I imagine is a rare taste of being under the radar.

I bang a right to head south on Fifth Street and notice how the evening is still holding tightly to late afternoon's muted light. *June.* "I always wish I could paint when I see the light out here," I say. "It makes it seem like I'm seeing things for the first time."

"I took a few watercolor classes and had to face the harsh reality that an enthusiastic finger painter does not an artist make," Arden says. "There's something about paintbrushes, though. I'm still drawn to them."

"Maybe you should be a makeup artist. That could be your calling."

"You never saw my paintings. Anyone who has wouldn't let me anywhere near a face."

Instead of stopping in front of Aunt Suebee's, I drive by and turn left onto Clark Street. I'm not ready to let the rest of the world in yet.

"Widow's Hole in all her glory," Arden says as we roll toward the dead end. "I never get tired of this place."

"No better place to watch the ferries crisscross," I say, turning off the engine.

"Pretty quiet down here too. Once Billy and I pretended we were running away and set up camp right over there. We didn't stay away long enough for anyone to even realize we were gone, but I'll never forget the thrill of planning our escape."

"Billy used to tell me his band was going to be called Widow's Hole," I say.

Arden turns to me, eyebrows raised. "Really? I never knew that. I didn't even know he had a band."

"He didn't. And he didn't play an instrument. Well, maybe air guitar. But he was great at naming things."

"Widow's Hole sounds pretty raunchy out of context," she says. "Out of this context, anyway." She motions toward the small basin sheltered by sandy beaches. It's a spectacular snapshot of Shelter Island, Greenport, and the bay.

"Last I heard, raunchy sells," I say.

There have been a few quasi-silent stretches on our drive east, moments void of conversation but filled with music from the radio or the hypnotic drone of traffic. The dark silence that wraps around us now has a different texture, heavy and unabridged.

"Are you thinking about Billy?"

"It's hard not to . . . being here," she says, sliding down in the seat and extending her right leg out the window. "I've been filling up my head with distractions—consciously and unconsciously—for days, but when I stop moving it catches up to me. That's when I remember he's not coming back."

I reach over for Arden's hand, not expecting her to grab mine so tightly. She turns her body toward me and makes a sour face. "I, uh, I need to tell you something. Something that will probably make you want to drive me home when you hear it, so I'm just gonna blurt it on out." This shift has come out of nowhere, and I brace myself for what's next. "There's something I haven't told you about Billy. We slept together. And not just once."

I open my mouth, but no sound comes out. I teeter between a shrug and a scream. Arden had been acting like a clueless preschooler on the playground when she actually knew how Billy felt, and she must've felt *something* for him, and not just once.

"Before you say anything, let me make this attempt to be honest—actually truthful. *I* slept with Billy. I mean, I'm the one who seduced him. He tried to fend me off every time, saying he didn't want the fucking to fuck up our friendship, and we should be careful about blurring the lines. Not that it was a challenge to wear his defenses down. I'd press my panties into his palm under the table, splash into the bay in my birthday suit, or just pour us each another shot and lean over to kiss him."

"Why are you telling me this, Arden? What exactly do you expect me to say?"

"I don't have any expectations. I just want you to know. I already feel like Billy's between us somehow—in a good way, mostly, but sometimes I feel like he's a wedge that will keep us apart."

Aunt Suebee once told me that when people show you their true colors, you shouldn't pretend not to see them. So what is Arden showing me? Is she a wounded, grieving woman trying to begin a new relationship without skeletons clanking around in her closet? Or does she thrive on drama and wreaking havoc?

"So when he told you he loved you and gave you the bracelet, you really *weren't* surprised, right?" I ask. It's painful to watch Arden shift in the seat, exposed.

"This is where you have to trust me. At least, I'm asking you to trust me. Billy and I were always drunk when we hooked up. It's not an excuse, but it does make everything blurry. I don't remember much and definitely have no memory of things we said to each other. We never talked about it afterward. We'd both pretend it never happened. Until the next time, anyway."

"So you thought you were two friends having a series of drunken flings and didn't realize Billy was storing up a powerhouse of emotion."

"I never analyzed what was going on between us."

"So when Clairebeth attacked you at the funeral home, those things she said, they must've stung."

"Stung. Yeah, they stung all right." Arden opens the truck door to swing her feet around.

"Where are you going?" I'm not in the mood to turn this conversation into a walk on the beach. I touch Arden's shoulder to spin her back. "Stay here. Let's finish this."

"I don't know what else to say. I think I should walk home. I don't want to talk about Billy and fucking Billy and fucking Billy up. I know you don't want to think about how you were *this close* to falling for a heartless bitch." I wrap my hand around the thumb and forefinger she's raised to show me just how close to the edge I've wandered.

"C'mere," I say, pulling her close so she can rest her head on my chest. There's only one thing I'm sure of—I don't want Arden to leave. She reminds me of the tide. Her confession may have dragged her away, but I can feel the sheer force of her washing ashore as she relaxes into me. We both know I'm making a choice. I'm going to take my chances.

When Arden tucks her head under my chin, I can't focus on anything beyond my intense physical attraction for her that's making it almost impossible for me to stay close to her without kissing her. I count the Shelter Island house windows being set ablaze by the setting sun, a fleeting illusion of flames before the day is extinguished. I watch a ferry glide toward Greenport and pretend I'm at the helm. I recite the alphabet from Z to A.

Except for the rhythmic rising and falling of her breath, Arden is so still I wonder if she's fallen asleep. I'm starting to doze myself. That's when she lifts her head to rub her face against mine. There is something so completely unexpected and innocent about the way she nuzzles me. I dig the fingers of my left hand into the seat to keep myself still, which becomes even more of a challenge when Arden brushes her lips above, around, and below mine. I look down, trying to memorize everything in my line of sight—the thick wave of hair that falls around Arden's face and the trail of freckles across the bridge of her nose.

"Let me know if I'm moving too fast for you," she whispers. And then everything escalates. Arden manages to straddle my lap without moving her lips from mine. I rake my fingers from her shoulder blades down to her waist.

"Those hands are going to be my downfall," she says. I grab her by the hips and then trace the outline of her waistband with my thumbs. Her skin is warm as I dip my thumbs down to find the top of her panties. The fabric is smooth, and I imagine shiny black fabric against her pale skin.

"You know why we're not fogging up the windows?" Arden asks, planting little kisses across my forehead. I shake my head, caught up in the sheer pleasure of her body pressing against me, and her face hovering above mine. "Because they're both rolled down, which makes for a bewitching cross breeze but means in your truck at Widow's Hole might not be the best place for us to get carried away." We share one more open-eyed kiss before she pulls away to climb back onto her side of the cab.

"Buy you a beer?" she asks with a sideways glance.

I don't have to follow her lead. If I do, I'll become an accomplice in allowing us to change lanes without looking over our shoulders. I'm all for living life looking through the windshield instead of the rearview mirror, but wouldn't veering away from Arden's confession only prolong an eventual crash? That must be why I say, "I thought you'd never ask," and drive to the Whiskey Wind before either one of us has a chance to change our mind.

When we walk through Whiskey Wind's Front Street door, I'm still reeling from being tangled up in Arden, and I have to concentrate on putting one foot in front of the other. It reminds me of how it feels to get my sea legs back. I didn't expect the place to be so packed on a Wednesday in June, and I am unsure if I'm prepared for yet another round of sensory overload.

Zeppelin's *Kashmir* wails from the jukebox, and I see a few arms raising shot glasses in the air at the end of the bar. That's when I spot Clairebeth shuffling toward us through the crowd. She throws her arms around me, practically dangling from my neck. I'm relieved that she's completely avoiding Arden. "What are you doing here? I can't believe you came to my show!"

"Your show? Since when do you have shows?" I look over where the only pool table in Greenport usually lives and see it's been pushed back to make room for Clairebeth's makeshift stage—amplifier, stool, guitar, music stands. There's also a small table with a pitcher of water and a glass.

Arden has learned a lot since her funeral home run-in and retreats into a conversation with Dinky, plumber by day and world's most belligerent dart enthusiast by night. He's trying to coax Arden into a game when I motion for her to stay where she is. Arden mouths "thank you" to me before deserting Dinky to head for the bathroom at the other side of the room.

"Hellooooo, earth to John," Clairebeth says, waving her hands in front of my face, "you're not listening to a word I'm saying, are you? Rude!"

"Guilty as charged. It's a little overwhelming in here."

"As I was *saying*, Captain John, I've been playing out for the last few months. How about . . ." Clairebeth pauses, obviously delighted by the question she's about to ask. "How about you open for me?"

I shake my head. "Thanks, but no thanks."

"C'mon, you haven't even checked out my fine-ass guitar. You're gonna freak. Not to mention I've always dreamed of having an opening act. And I even have a request."

"And what might that be?" I ask, almost afraid to hear her answer.

"Duh. *Get in Line*," she says. "You really don't pay attention, do you? C'mon. The natives are getting restless. Pretty soon they'll only want to sing along with Guns 'N Roses on the jukebox, and then I'll really be screwed."

I shake my head again as this larger-than-life woman stares me down and walks over to the bar. When's the last time I'd played to a room? I can't even remember. Maybe I need to jump into the eye of the hurricane if I want to come out intact, and Whiskey Wind is definitely frenetic tonight. The thought of singing for Arden makes my head buzz, not to mention that keeping Clairebeth content and far away from her is probably not a bad idea.

I search the crowd for Arden, but she's hidden somewhere in the pulsing room. I order a Heineken and give Clairebeth a thumbs up. I don't know why I'm surprised to find Clairebeth's guitar tuned, but it is yet another unexpected moment in the handful of hours since I'd stepped off the *Alanna Rose*.

I switch on the mic and dive in. "Well, it's Wednesday night at the Whiskey Wind, and I have a confession to make," I pause as the room quiets down enough. "It's been *way* too long since my last show, and I want to thank the Clairebeth Mickelson for inviting me to open for her. Her request is a song that clearly shows just how fucked up someone's attempt at having a love life can be. Yes, I can attest to the fact that truth is stranger than fiction, and I was even stupid enough to capture my miserable story in a song so I can relive it for all eternity." There's a rumble of laughter, and I look up to see Clairebeth deep in conversation with a guy who knows her well enough to brush the hair out of her eyes. Arden has surfaced and moves up closer to settle in with her back against a video game. She watches me with a half smile. Nothing like laying out the pathetic landscape of my love life for her in a matter of minutes. That's just the kind of guy I am.

Chapter Twenty-Five: Arden

Wednesday, June 1, 1994

Seeing Clairebeth is like walking into a snowbank. I unfreeze long enough to escape into a meaningless conversation with dart-happy Dinky, and I am grateful to find a low profile spot next to a video game.

And then I see John, getting ready to perform. I'm having a hard time concentrating on him. On anything, really. Everything around me seems mixed up and loud. I wonder if John can read my expression, but he seems completely caught up in his song.

Someone elbows my side. Clairebeth. "This your hideout?" she asks.

I don't respond. She doesn't budge.

"I've always loved this song," she continues. "And *driftlove*? That word fucking rocks. You may not pick up on it the first time around, but it's in one of the last verses. That word needs to be in the dictionary. I demand it. In fact, I'm gonna nominate it for word-dom. What do you think?" She lifts her bottle for a toast, but when I raise mine she pulls hers away before the clink. "I will *never* forgive you, Arden. And why don't you stop stringing John along? You know he's not good enough for you either, and you've done enough damage around here." She brushes by me to stand closer to the stage.

Having somehow managed to survive Hurricane Claire, my anxiety still accelerates. Is this what a panic attack feels like? It's as if I've been stapled to the floor and a vengeful vacuum has sucked all the air out of the room. The only thing I can do is focus on the rhythm of John's song, and I'm relieved when a wave of applause signals that he'll be on his way back to me. John will get me out of here.

Then Clairebeth saunters up to the mic. "Not so fast," she says into it. "Did you really think you could get away with just one, Captain John Raymond?"

John nods his head as he places her guitar back on its stand. "I think I need some audience participation to bring him back," Clairebeth says, clapping her hands. Soon the whole room is applauding and whistling. I know it's over when a few voices start chanting, "John, John, John."

I think my face is expressionless, but hell, I could be smiling at this point. I want John to see what's going on beneath my surface, to sense that I'm starting to unhinge. And then my expectation morphs into irrational anger when he's unable to read my mind. John winks at me and walks back toward Clairebeth. I'm on my own.

"What do you have in mind?" John asks.

"I have an unspoken rule that I *never* start a set with something slow," she says. "But, I also believe rules are made to be broken. Just like hearts. And some of us in the room know more about that than others." A rowdy "I hear that!" rises up from the crowd as she continues, "So how 'bout 'See Your Face'? It's short, and it's about as sad and sweet as it gets."

John nods in agreement. When the first words come out of his mouth, I feel like he's inviting the entire room to stare at me with accusing eyes. Doesn't he realize that I can't listen to a song like this?

"We've been friends for so long," he sings. "I loved you long before you knew. Through the years we've grown together. It hurts so bad so far from you." Clairebeth sings the next few lines, and then they lean into the mic together for, "I just want to see your face."

I'm not sure how I get from Point A—hyperventilating by a video game—to Point B—the Adams Street sidewalk behind Whiskey Wind—but that's where I land, my head tucked between my knees like I'm preparing for a plane to crash.

Later, when I try to sort through that moment and remember my exit, I think about the time a cop found my friend Ben wandering along the highway not far from an accident site. Several cars had piled up in a nasty crash, and Ben was asking all kinds of questions about what had happened. It took a few minutes for the officer to figure out Ben was one of the crash victims. His car had ended up in a ditch on the side of the road, and he'd smacked his head on the steering wheel. Ben told me he later learned that lots of people die that way—wandering into traffic in a postaccident daze. I can't even begin to piece together what had happened to me inside the bar, but I feel like I'm covered in tire treads.

Is it really only a few moments later that I hear John's voice beside me, saying he'd stopped playing when he saw me drop my beer bottle on the floor and run toward the back door?

"Take me home," I say. "Will you? Now?" I don't move, even though part of me aches to lean into him. I stay tucked up, like I'm poised to somersault home if that's what it'll take to get me there. I even start silently counting the number of blocks between Adams Street and my front porch.

"Are you sick, Arden? What's going on?"

"I don't know and I do know, all at the same time. I guess it's more like I don't want to know.

He slips his arm around my shoulders, and I know he'll keep it there as long as I him need to.

"I never really paid attention when people would say, 'Timing is everything,' but now I feel like there's this neon sign flashing right in front of my face, taunting me. *Timing is everything. Timing is everything.* Fucking sign."

A few people wobble out onto the sidewalk, not noticing us planted outside the door. "Sorry, man," one of them says as he steps on John's hand.

"No worries," John says without looking up. "So, you were saying, timing is everything."

For better or worse, he's paying attention. "You. And me. The timing just isn't right," I continue. I can feel his body tense up, but he doesn't back away from me.

"Is this about you telling me that you and Billy slept together? We don't have to sort through all that right now."

"You have no idea what you're talking about. I just scared the hell out myself in there. I was paralyzed. Maybe I'm having a panic attack. I don't know. There's something going on that I'm not ready to face, and when I'm with you I feel like someone's turned on the bathroom light, and I have to examine every pore of my life. It's what you do to me. Some other time I'd probably be inspired by the raw honesty of it all, but right now I just want to hide in the dark."

"*You* opened up to *me*. You had the courage to do that, and I'm not walking away." Am I imagining it or is his arm barely resting on my shoulders now? Is he loosening his grip?

"I'm trying to warn you, John. I'm a mess."

"No, what you're doing is making a mess of things right now. Fuck, Arden. I'm human. *You're* human. We're human."

"I'm human and crazy. I think I'm losing my mind. I see what I've done, the kind of person I've been. Not just with Billy, but with my friend Casey. And with my mom. Steer clear, would you? Don't wait for a disaster."

I hear John take a few slow breaths. "You know, the Houston Ship Channel used to be the only place in the world to get into a game of Texas Chicken, but I think we're playing it right here. On the surface, it's all water pressure and physics, but deep down, it's really about faith. The channel isn't very wide, so when two deep-draft ships are going to meet and need to pass, they steer directly at each other as though they'll have a head-on collision. At the last possible moment, they each swerve right and let hydro physics do the rest. A wall of water acts like a cushion between them and keeps the two vessels from colliding."

I don't know what makes me sadder, the fact I've totally gotten sucked into John's description and am already missing all the stories I'll never hear, or that I'm too exhausted from the inside out to want to listen to him explain that our relationship is like a game of Texas Chicken.

"Arden, we've been moving toward each other head-on since the day we met at Billy's wake. And now, you're focusing on the potential disaster of getting too close. And it *is* fucking scary. But I want to trust in us and who we are to be the wall of water that will keep us just far enough apart."

"I can't trust in that, John. I don't want to open up right now. I want to hibernate, to shut down. I want to be alone. And I think I let things like our connection to Billy and *through* Billy accelerate how I feel about you. You're not Billy."

"I'm not Billy," he repeats.

"And when I heard you sing that song with Clairebeth, it wound me up. Didn't you realize how those lyrics would crush me? I thought you got it. That you got me. I was wrong, and that song was a wake-up call. I just want to see Billy's face. I want to apologize for giving him so many parts of me except the one he'd been waiting for, the one that mattered. I want him to know there's no way in the world I would ever turn my back on him. And I need you to know that I am incapable of loving anyone."

John stands and grabs my hand to pull me up along with him. "Is this some sort of test? To see if I'm the kind of person—the kind of guy—who steers clear of anything complicated?"

"Complicated?" I sigh. "This has absolutely nothing to do with testing you. It has nothing to do with you at all. In fact, right now I can't even look at you without thinking about Billy, and *that* is fucked up."

"*This* is fucked up," John says, not letting go of my hand. "You're going to walk away from us, just like that."

"What I'm doing is not walking away from Billy's memory. I could focus on how good it feels to be around you, but the twisted part is that being with you is like holding onto a piece of Billy too. At least, that's how it feels to me right now. And don't act like you're in prime relationship shape either. You're married to the sea and have been running back to her for years so you don't ever have to take a good look at the rest of your life."

"Nice. Where the hell did that come from?"

"Observation." My tongue is dry and swollen.

"Maybe if we stand here long enough, you'll realize grieving isn't linear or logical, and that when someone is absolutely crazy about you he doesn't care if you have it all figured out. You will *never* have it all figured out. Who does?"

When I don't respond, he leans over to touch the side of his forehead to mine. "Please don't be afraid of getting too close."

I hadn't wanted to say it out loud, but it's the only thing I have left. "I just can't bear to be around you anymore. I want to go home." Silence. "Should I walk?"

John doesn't answer but drops my hand and marches across the parking lot to open his truck's passenger door. When I walk toward him, his face softens as if he's watching me walk down the aisle with the promise of forever between us instead of hurrying to leave him behind.

John's expression upsets me. "This isn't some momentary lapse of reason," I say. "It's over. And I'm sorry. I wish I could rewind to that first day in my apartment and realize what was really going on with me." I also knew there wasn't a centrifuge on earth powerful enough to separate the confusing mass of sadness and loss I felt when I thought about Billy.

"Don't worry," John says, reminding me I am still here, tangled. "I understand you, Arden. And I don't need to rewind to that first day, because there isn't a moment of it I'll ever forget. I *did* see what was really happening, but I'm not going to rewrite history and pretend this uncharted territory isn't exactly where we both need to be."

Is John crazy enough to feel hopeful? Maybe he isn't rewriting history, but he is letting his heart tell the story. I feel a sudden wave of nausea when John turns on to Bridge Street, and I worry that I might throw up before I make it home. The night doesn't need a physical exclamation mark, so I shut my eyes and focus on taking small, short breaths through my mouth. I don't wait for John to say anything as I scramble out the door and onto my porch. All I want to do is curl up in my bed and turn off the light.

Chapter Twenty-Six: John

Wednesday, June 8, 1994

I expect Arden to look back after she jumps out of the truck and runs toward her porch. She doesn't. I stay there for a few minutes after she shuts off the porch light, stunned and in the dark in more ways than one. *Fuck.* I know it's time to leave when I start getting angry that the fireflies actually have the nerve to act like there's something to light up about.

I drive straight back to the city and don't leave my apartment for a few days. Every time the phone rings, I'm sure it's going to be Arden. I slip into a routine of eating bowl after bowl of cereal, watching game shows, and drifting in and out of patchy, restless sleep.

And yes, I call Arden several times a day. Every. Single. Day. She doesn't answer her city number, and when I dial Greenport, her mom pretends to write down a message, speaking in a voice that's a little too loud and polite. "I'm not sure when to expect her, John, but I'll be sure to tell her that you called. She has your number, right?" *She has my number all right,* I think. *She has all of me.*

I wonder what's going on with Garrett and even consider calling Chase to find out but can't bear the thought of hearing his voice.

I finally get the only other call I've been waiting for. It's from a captain looking to get off the boat early. I'm grateful for this small measure of relief.

A few hours later, I'm at the helm of the *Lucy Reinauer*, imagining what it would be like to bring Arden up into the wheelhouse. I know she'd love the expanse of it all. Even when a tugboat's tied up, everything seems wide open from up there, like you're inhabiting an essay question where you can show what you know instead of being trapped in a multiple-choice test that tries to make you believe things that matter have only one answer.

I press my right palm against my face as I shake my head. I've suspended Arden in the future tense. No matter what she said or felt or didn't feel, I can't stop believing that someday this will all be part of our story.

I sit down with my guitar, already knowing which song I need to sing. As much as I hope Arden will find her way back to me, I also know I'll have to change course if I'm ever going to really let her in. Could I find the courage to stop hiding behind the ruthless, demanding lover that rocked me to sleep every night? How much longer am I going to deny that having a purpose on the tug made it easier for me to not do what really mattered to me?

As I tune my guitar, I marvel at the luminous abalone sky and think about how I could describe it to Arden. That's when I start whispering *someday* aloud. It's the mantra I've been clinging to all week. Will I ever get to tell Arden about the silver-pink iridescence radiating upward from the horizon—better yet, show it to her? If I focus on *someday*, the hopeful rhythm of its rising and falling, there's no way I'll stop believing that someday I just might.

Chapter Twenty-Seven: Arden

Wednesday, June 8, 1994

The screen door slams behind me, propelling me inside with a decisiveness I lack. What if a breeze followed me up the porch steps, blowing the door open just enough to give me a reason to turn and pull it shut? Could the glow of John's headlights have lured me back outside and transformed me into the fearless moth I'd almost become—an instinctual creature unafraid to fly toward the unknown?

But no, I've been ambushed by darkness. My parents' back door is always unlocked, but since they don't know I'm in Greenport I have to taxi through the kitchen without the dim nightlight by the stairs to brighten my runway to the liquor cabinet. I squat down in front of the sliding doors, feeling the rough fabric of Dad's recliner on my right arm as I reach into the depths of the bottle brigade. My fingers brush over the squat Crown Royal and slender SoCo until they find Absolut's smooth cap and familiar silhouette tucked in the back row.

Even though I know my mind is racing too fast for sleep to catch me, I focus on the mission at hand—escaping to my bed so the night can begin to end. I cradle the Absolut like a football, not bothering to pit stop for ice or a glass. The thought of pouring something exhausts me. Tilting the bottle back will require enough effort.

Around 5 a.m., I stop replaying choppy sequences from the last twelve hours and switch gears to finding my way back to the city. I make my bed and splash cold water on my face, remembering to grab my small Wm. J. Mills canvas bag before attempting an undetected escape. I walk toward the bus stop without bothering to shuffle through the takeout-menu-stuffed kitchen drawer for a bus schedule. I arrive just in time to watch a gobstopper sun bob up onto the horizon, oozing strips of sherbet orange and pink light above the empty bay.

"This is what it feels like to lose a game of Texas Chicken," I whisper aloud as the bus rumbles up and stops with a tired whine. *I'm retreating to my corner.* No one will know I didn't trust the physics of love, didn't trust myself. And no one would believe that over the course of a few short weeks everything about the landscape of my life has been chopped up and laid out in an unrecognizable pattern.

The monotony of the bus ride and my walk from 39th and Third to my apartment lulls me into accepting that starting over might seem impossible, but it's my only option. And then I open my apartment door. *Of course, the radio.* It's still sitting on my desk, the last to know that it's no longer a conduit connecting two hearts.

I stare at the radio like I'm examining a pet that's just learned a curious new trick, trying to figure out what to do next. It isn't as simple as burying an old lover's T-shirt in the back of a drawer. I decide to cover it with a dishtowel and wait for inspiration.

The next day, I dive in and start swimming on the surface of my old life, staying afloat thanks to frenzied projects and cocktails with anyone who's around and thirsty. It isn't until a week later that a whisper wakes me from a sweaty, dreamless sleep just as dawn is about to unwrap a new day. *Call John.* It's less epiphany and more that the two words gnawing at me finally latching onto a lucid nerve. *Hadn't I learned anything from losing Billy?* I'd slammed another door shut, and now John is going to be out on a tug with a chasm of hurt between us.

I'm not sure how that early-morning dream turns into me banging on John's apartment door with a booming voice startling me. "If you're looking for John, he's gone," it says. The voice belongs to an old woman in a lavender velour bathrobe who stands in the hall outside the apartment next door, stroking a very large, loud-purring cat.

"Oh," I say without moving.

"Should be back in two weeks or so." She leans forward to whisper in her cat's ear as she steps back inside and the door clicks shut.

When I get back to my apartment, I keep the lights off and walk over to the windows to gaze down at the flecks of light on the river below. *I'm being irrational and need to stick with my original plan—one foot in front of the other.*

That's when it hits me—a bright white light moves across my face and continues on to illuminate the room through the windows next to me. My heart gallops. *John.*

John had told me about the time he found out the owner of his tug company was celebrating his birthday at The River Café in Brooklyn. John had maneuvered his tug in close to the restaurant to shine a huge spotlight on the owner. Then he laid on the horn, and the crowd inside the restaurant went wild. The owner basked in the attention, his ego lit up even brighter than the flood of light filling the room. "So you see, when I want someone's attention, I'll go any lengths to get it." *Is he trying to get mine tonight?*

The light moves back and forth in broad sweeps. Grabbing the binoculars I keep on the bookcase, I rush back to the windows, wondering if the *Alanna Rose* will come into focus.

That's when I remember Billy's decision making advice: Toss a coin, and in the brief moment it lingers in the air, you'll know how you want it to land.

By the time my binoculars reveal that a Coast Guard ship, not the *Alanna Rose*, is responsible for casting the wide funnel of light on my building, I realize that the light is my coin, and I exhale into knowing how I wanted it to land. I think about John in the wheelhouse and decide to go for a long walk along the East River so I can look up at the sea of stars that wink above us both.

* * *

Songbook
unless otherwise noted,
all songs written at sea by Joshua Horton

Prologue | Big Swell

Big swell rolling through the sea
tumbling on the beach.
Big swell rolling through the ocean
big swell don't mean that much to me.

Maybe you do, but I'm going anyway
just a small man on the ocean.
I've got things I've got to tow across the sea,
big swell have mercy on me.
I said, big swell have mercy on me.

Big swell if you show no mercy,
and keep me for yourself,
everything I told to my fine love
would make a lying man of me.

I told her how you fill me with purpose,
told her how you rock me to sleep.
I told her out here I don't need control,
I just set my course and let all be.

I can't stay out here with you forever,
growing old before my time.
I need to spend some time in my fine baby's arms
and she needs to spend some in mine.

Big swell rolling through the sea
tumbling on the beach.
Big swell rolling through the ocean
big swell have mercy on me. . . .{repeats}

Chapter 2 | Coolest Boy

I roll with my friends, all around town
talkin' all kinds of shit about getting out
about getting out of this town.
They roll with me to the package store.
Cause they know I know all the older guys
so we can score some beers,
just to take us out of this world.

{Chorus}

Cause I'm the single most—coolest boy, all right in this town.
Cause I'm the single most—coolest boy, yes in this town.

Down by the tracks, we fuck with the trains
throwing rusted cans and rocks and then we just
smoke out our brains, smoke 'em clear out
yes, smoke 'em clear out of this world.
There's no time for school . . . I've got things to do
like stuff and things and other stuff
and just lots of things to do.
And brother it ain't easy . . . it ain't easy being cool.

{Chorus—variation}

And I'm the single most—coolest boy, oh yes in this town.
I say don't ask me why cause I'll cap you clear in your left eye
Yes, I'm the coolest boy in this town.
Cause I'm the single most—coolest boy, oh yes in this town.

{Bridge}

I don't need no one to be pissed off at.
I've things on my mind—you ain't got the time
and all you motherfuckers is whack.
Don't none of ya . . . don't none of ya know nothing.
That's why I've got a plan. I'm gonna be a marine,
a mean fighting machine. I'll come back to town and stroll
around with my dress blues on, and you'll see that I'm the
coolest boy that ever made it out of this town.

{Chorus—variation}

Cause I'm the single most—coolest boy, oh yes in this town.
Cause I'm the single most—coolest boy, yes in this town.

Chapter 3 | Amazing Grace

Verses written by John Newton & music from the traditional song
"New Britain," joined to lyrics by composer William Walker

Amazing grace, how sweet the sound,
That saved a wretch like me.
I once was lost but now am found.
Was blind, but now I see.

'Twas grace that taught my heart to fear.
And Grace my fears relieved.
How precious did that grace appear
the hour I first believed.

Amazing grace, how sweet the sound,
That saved a wretch like me.
I once was lost but now am found.
Was blind, but now I see.

Chapter 8 | Cold October Evening

That cold October evening
blows the wind against the rocks.
Seems my most recent saddest memories
linger 'round these battered docks.

Now I wonder if it's raining
like it always does out there.
And if it always does—I guess it is.
Guess I'm glad to be right here.

She damn sure knew I was a sailor.
She seemed to like it at the time.
I always called and wrote and mailed her.
Sung her songs in perfect time.

She said 'I'll love you forever'
said she'd always be true.
But I just wish I was aware of—
she ain't mean me, she meant you.

That cold October evening
blows the wind against the rocks.
Seems my most recent saddest memories
walk the nights of these haunted docks.

And I'm inside this goddamned wheelhouse
while the ghost of her love sways,
but I'm looking out to harbor lights.
It's time, it's time . . .
It's time this cold October evening's under way.

{Chorus}

Chapter 12 | Louisiana Skies

Pretty lady from Baton Rouge
Come chase away my New York blues
Sweet lady—your sweet song
You belong in my arms.

Sunshine eyes and golden brown hair
makes me feel so good
and takes me there next to you—Baton Rouge
sweet lady—sweet song

{Chorus}

Louisiana skies are blue
breezy eyes of my Baton Rouge
sweet lady—sweet song
You belong in my arms.

Cajun Queen in Bayou LaFourche
spice of life and words so true
sweet lady—sweet songs
You belong in my arms.

{Chorus. Repeat chorus.}

Whisper 'cross the bay
feel the wind come through my heart
makes me want to stay
and I feel like—when I feel I'm all alone
I think of you and Baton Rouge
Take me home to my

Louisiana skies are blue
breezy eyes of my Baton Rouge
sweet lady—sweet song
You belong in my arms.

{Chorus. Repeat chorus.}
You belong in my arms.

Chapter 15 | Long Island Sailor

These winter nights can sure be long.
Man, I wonder what time it is over there.
But damn girl, your hands are strong
pushing through my hair.

I almost slipped and broke my heart
out in the icy cold.
I thank you for reminding me
that it's time, it's time to move along. I said,

{Chorus 1}

"Ain't no lady worth bellyaching for
when you're a Long Island sailor on the Jersey Shore.
Ain't no memory worth bellyaching for
when you're a Long Island sailor on the Jersey Shore."

Last night I was out in a storm.
Man, them waves threw back some memories
of a girl that I knew one week and three years before.

But we crossed that Manasquan bar, I threw my lines ashore to
Olivia, she laid my troubles down,
Lindsey and Holly passed my heart around. We said,

{Chorus 2}

"Ain't no lady worth mes-morizing for
when you're a Long Island sailor on the Jersey Shore.

Ain't no memory worth bellyaching for
when you're a Long Island sailor on the Jersey Shore."

You say you'd like to take a wintry walk.
Yeah, I'd like to do that.
Down the beach, while the wind's laid low
in that air, so crisp
I said you're holding me oh so tight. I said,

{Chorus 1}

Chapter 18 | Hitch My Soul

Fourth of July and I'm cold and I'm tired.
This summer ain't gone nowhere but wrong.
Ninety degrees, but inside I'm just freezin'
from standing still for far too long.

{Chorus}

I'm gonna hitch my soul, hitch my soul,
hitch my soul to your train.
Hitch my soul, hitch my soul,
hitch my soul to your train.

Out of a dark sky a shadow of kindness
gently reached out its hand.
It threw a white light into the heart of my poisoned soul
and I knew right there and then

{Chorus}

{Bridge}

I've walked through darkness and called it desire.
Brokenheartedness had long been a friend of mine.
But how you move me is something I've never known.
But that don't matter girl 'cause
I'm never ever ever gonna let you go, no . . .

{Chorus}

I've walked through shadows
and the puddles of a bleeding heart.
Happy to be sad, to be being used.
And then I saw you looking at me
as I saw myself looking right back at you.

{Chorus}

{Bridge}

{Chorus}

Chapter 24 | Get in Line

Broke again in Memphis with a hard one tied on.
I think that train to Texas I was supposed to ride on.
Last night I was a daddy in a fastback Ford.
Today I'm bummin' a smoke off some riverbank whore
She said

{Chorus}

Get in that line, she said get in line, go get in that line,
just get in line, she said get in line, go get in that line,
g-g-g-get in that line, she said get in line. Said, you want
somethin' different, better get yourself to the end of the line.

Scored me a job in New York for that high dollar pay,
I called my olive-eyed baby, said, "I'll pick you up at JFK."
She said, "I miss you so much, suga',
something you need to know. See I married a marine
out in San Diego, go, go, go . . ."

{Chorus 2}

Get in that line, she said get in line, go get in that line,
just get in line, she said get in line, go get in that line,
g-g-g-get in that line, she said get in line. Said, you want
some of your girl? Better get yourself to the end of the line.

Found me a piece of driftlove in that fine Puget Sound
Who thought I'd find something so fine just floating around?
A sunshine girl to keep my world in constant rotation,
she liked it wild in that French style—wait, man,
I was away on vacation!

{Repeat Chorus 2}

So I'm driving across the country in my old GMC.
Seemed like this whole trip, man, I'd just been riding on "E."
I pulled into a juke joint wondering why I even bother.
Got locked outta my truck while I was stealing a look
from some whore in Nevada. She said

Get in that line, she said get in line, go get in that line, go
get in that line, she said get in line, go get in that line,
go get in that line, she said get in line. Said, you want
somethin' different, better get yourself to the end of the line.

Chapter 25 | See Your Face

You and me, we've been friends for so long.
I loved you long before you knew.
And through the years we've grown together
it hurts so bad so far from you. I said,
said it hurts so bad so far from you.

We sleep ten thousand miles distant,
and we don't share much in our days.
But you know that I'm always here to listen,
so now listen to me.
Something's missing if I can't see your face
Hear what I said, something's missing if I can't see your face
Hear me cryin', something's missing if I can't see your face,
your face—*that's right.*

I just want to see your face.
I just want to see your face.
And I just want to see your face.

{Repeat}

Chapter 26 | Heart of a Sailor

I'm sittin' by the roadside, waiting for my train
a breeze off the river chills me, applauds my goin' away
'cause I'm thinking 'bout my home,
kissed my girl good-bye in her sleep.
I'm headin' back to my boat, goin' back to sea.

My life is stuffed in a sea bag. My dwelling's a musty rack.
When I sleep I've got the stars above and the sea below my back.

I'm just a sailor and I'm torn between the tides, the raging sea
that's got a hold of me, and a woman on my mind.

Years of comin' and goin', I'm like a squall in a southern bay.
I jump into your life and churn it up,
then gone in that same day.
Locked up in a treasure chest cast of solid lead where I stow
my fears, my deepest thoughts, and these things that I can't forget.
Because a seaman's life is love or else inside I'd surely die.
Laid out with the sea below me, above the starry sky.

I'm just a sailor and if it wasn't all I knew,
I'd come ashore through the rollin' surf to try to be with you.

I'm just a sailor and if it wasn't all I knew,
I'd come ashore through the rolling surf to try to be with you.

As I'm sittin' beside the tracks and thinkin' about these things
I know damn well that if I stay 'round here
what tomorrow brings.
In this sea of concrete shadows with the busy and confused
just workin' for a dollar, just workin' and being used.

Well, my life is one of chances.
I count my blessings in the wind.
'Cause the sea is deeper than your love
and her love is deeper than all sin.

I'm just a sailor, born to take the tide
so when ya ask me why I'm goin' now,
I'm a sailor, that's why.

I'm just a sailor and if it wasn't all I knew,
I'd come ashore through the rolling surf to try to be with you.

Anchored in gratitude . . .

I am indebted to my family—thank you for being my True North and a constant source of love and inspiration.

I am tremendously grateful for my friends who know the song in my heart and sing it back to me when I need to remember the words.

I am thankful for each early reader whose feedback helped THE WHEELHOUSE CAFÉ evolve into this dream come true.

Thornton Wilder said, "We can only be said to be alive in those moments when our hearts are conscious of our treasures."

In this moment, I have never felt more alive.

Thank you.

About the Author

Yvonne Lieblein is a writer, creative producer, and business strategist from the seaside village of Greenport, New York. Inspired by songs her husband composed while at sea in the 1990s, Yvonne wrote THE WHEELHOUSE CAFÉ and fulfilled her lifelong dream of pairing a story with music.

The Wheelhouse Café
Book Club Discussion Starters

How do the circumstances of John and Arden's initial encounter affect their relationship? Which relationships in your own life have been especially influenced by the way they began?

Why do you think Arden's feelings for Chase dissipate when she meets John?

When you read about John's life at sea, what appeals to you and why?

John says he feels most at home in the wheelhouse. Where do you feel most at home?

Why do Arden's unresolved relationships with Casey and Billy haunt her as she gets closer to John?

How do you think Clairebeth's accusations and volatile behavior affect Arden's sense of guilt?

THE WHEELHOUSE CAFÉ begins in mid-May and ends on June 8. Can you recall a period in your life when momentous events or revelations occurred within a short timespan?

Do you think there will be another chapter in John and Arden's love story?

How did the music affect how you experienced THE WHEELHOUSE CAFÉ?

Where is *your* Wheelhouse Café – the place or circumstance where you express yourself freely whether or not you're heard or understood?

For sales, editorial information, subsidiary rights information or a
catalog, please write or phone or e-mail
IBOOKS
Manhanset House
Dering Harbor, New York
US Sales: 1-800-68-BRICK Tel: 212-427-7139
BrickTowerPress.com
ibooksinc.com
bricktower@aol.com

www.Ingram.com

For sales in the UK and Europe please contact our distributor,
Gazelle Book Services
White Cross Mills
Lancaster, LA1 4XS,
UK Tel: (01524) 68765 Fax: (01524) 63232 email:
jacky@gazellebooks.co.uk

CPSIA information can be obtained at www.ICGtesting.com
Printed in the USA
BVOW06s1226140716

455212BV00005B/19/P